CASE FOR GRACE FOR KIDS

Other books in the Lee Strobel series for kids:

Case for Christ for Kids, Updated and Expanded

Case for Faith for Kids, Updated and Expanded

Case for a Creator for Kids, Updated and Expanded

Case for Christ for Kids 90-Day Devotional

New York Times Bestselling Author

LEE STROBEL

with Jesse Florea

CASE FOR GRACE FOR KIDS

ZONDERKIDZ

Case for Grace for Kids

This title is also available as a Zondervan ebook. Visit www.zondervan.com/ebooks.

Requests for information should be addressed to:

Zondervan, *3900 Sparks Drive SE, Grand Rapids, Michigan 49546*

ISBN 978-0-310-73656-1

Cover design: Deborah Washburn
Interior design and composition: Carlos Eluterio Estrada and Greg Johnson
Illustrations © Terry Colon

Printed in the United States of America

15 16 17 18 19 20 /DCI/ 21 20 19 18 17 16 15 14 13 12 11 10 9 8 7 6 5 4 3 2 1

For Abigail, Penelope, Brighton, and Oliver.

God's gifts of grace.

TABLE OF CONTENTS

"Therefore, if anyone is in Christ,
the new creation has come:
The old has gone, the new is here!"

— 2 Corinthians 5:17

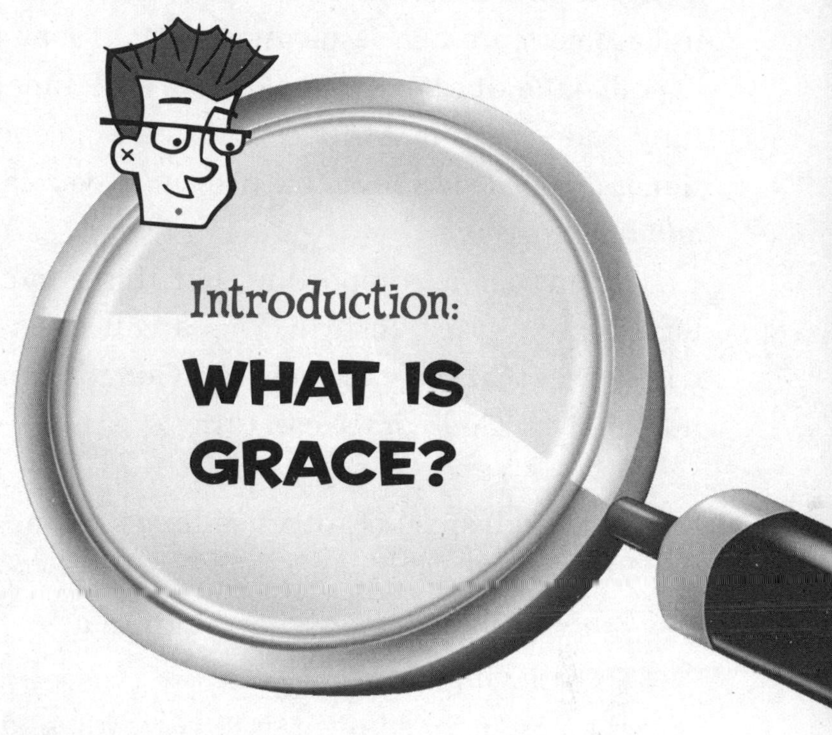

Introduction: WHAT IS GRACE?

Maybe you've heard grace defined by the popular acrostic:

God's

Riches

At

Christ's

Expense

To put it even more simply, "Grace is the favor shown by God to sinners."[1] Grace gives to us the ability to have a relationship with God, brings us into his family, and provides the power to become more like Jesus. As easy as it may be to define the word *grace*, it can take a lifetime to fully understand it. At its core it is an unconditional gift of God's love that we can never earn and don't deserve.

Definitions are important, but this is not a textbook on grace. Instead, it is a collection of true stories that show the power of God to change human lives. God's grace can turn:

- a reckless rebel into a selfless servant of God;
- a regular thirteen-year-old into a lifesaving hero;
- an abandoned orphan into one of God's precious children;
- and a mass murderer into a forgiven and powerful church planter.

This book talks about a very personal journey for me to solve the riddle of grace. Along the way, I found evidence I couldn't ignore of God's grace working in the lives of kids and adults all over the world.

These true accounts of people whose lives are so fantastic can only be explained as the work of a gracious God. As you read these stories, I want you to think. But not like you can't remember an important fact on a test or when you're puzzling over a difficult problem in math class. I want you to think like a detective about what each story shows you of God's character … and maybe how you've seen this exact kind of grace in your own life. In each of these stories, you'll find a piece to the grace puzzle that shows:

- how grace goes beyond forgiveness to acceptance and even adoption by God;
- how it brings back hope when none is left;
- and how it lets us forgive those who hurt us — and even find forgiveness for ourselves.

In other words, you will find the truths all of us need for the lives that God wants for us.

Christ is unique among world religions, and so is the grace he offers. Sometimes, to understand grace, we need to see it described rather than merely defined. After all, the Bible is one huge story about grace. When Jesus wanted his followers to fully feel the emotional impact of grace, he told the story of a Prodigal Son.[2]

So here are stories for you. Through these other people's experiences, I trust you will see your story as well.

Chapter 1
ON THE CASE

PUTTING TOGETHER THE PUZZLE OF GRACE

I grew up in an upscale neighborhood northwest of Chicago. My dad worked hard to build his business and provide everything we needed and more — as far as material things were concerned. He loved my mom. And everybody in the neighborhood seemed to like him.

Still, my relationship with him was always frosty, but not in a cool snowman-like way. It was cold. Maybe I needed more positive comments than the other kids. I don't know. He didn't take me to Cub Scouts, cheer at my Little League games, watch my speech tournaments, or go to my graduations.

Over time, I learned that the only way to get his attention was through winning things. So I strived for good grades, was elected president of my school, was the editor of the school newspaper, and even wrote stories for the community paper. Still, I don't remember any positive words coming from my dad. Not one.

I do remember, however, once when I was a kid, the entire family went to church together. We did this fairly regularly. But after the service on this particular Sunday, my dad drove everyone home — but he forgot to bring me. I can still picture my panic as I searched wildly around the church, looking for my family. My heart pounded, and my hope sank as I realized my father had left me behind.

It was a mistake on his part, but it was difficult for me not to see it as symbolic of how our relationship was developing.

One evening when I was about twelve years old, my father and I fought over something. I

WHAT'S IN A NAME?

You'll find random facts about grace sprinkled throughout this book. For instance, did you know *Grace* is one of the most popular names for girls in the United States? From 2003–2006, *Grace* ranked in the Top 20 of all girls' names. And nearly every year, *Grace* breaks into the Top 30.[3]

How many Graces do you know?

walked away feeling shame and guilt. I went to bed vowing to try to behave better, to be more obedient, to somehow make myself more acceptable to my dad. I can't recall the details of what caused our conflict that evening, but what happened next is still vivid in my mind.

I dreamed I was making myself a sandwich in the kitchen when a luminous angel suddenly appeared and started telling me about how wonderful and glorious heaven is. I listened for a while then said matter-of-factly, "I'm going there," which I meant, of course, at the end of my life.

The angel's reply stunned me. "How do you know?"

How do I know? What kind of question is that? "Well, uh, I've tried to be a good kid," I stammered. "I've tried to do what my parents say. I've tried to behave. I've been to church."

"That doesn't matter," the angel said.

Now I was staggered. How could it *not* matter — all my efforts to do the right thing, to be dutiful, to live up to the demands of my parents and teachers? Panic rose inside me. Words wouldn't come out of my mouth.

The angel let me stew for a few moments. Then he said, "Someday, you'll understand." Instantly, he was gone.

I woke up in a sweat. It's the only dream I remember from my childhood. Through the years it would come to mind every once in a while, and yet I would always shake it off. It was just a dream.

As I got older, I found myself getting more confused about heaven and spiritual matters. When I became a teenager, my parents insisted that I attend Bible classes at the church.

"But I'm not sure I even believe that stuff," I told my dad.

His response was stern: "Go. You can ask questions there."

But questions were only reluctantly tolerated during class. And the answers I did receive only scratched the surface. Nobody seemed willing to dig in and understand how deep their faith was. I actually emerged from those classes with more doubts than when I started.

Doubts continued to annoy me as I grew and my teachers insisted that science had explained away God. A creator was no longer needed. I became increasingly doubtful. Something was missing — in my family and in my soul — that created a gnawing need I couldn't even describe at the time.

Years later, I was driving down Northwest Highway in Palatine, Illinois, when I flipped on the radio. I can still recall the exact location, the time of day, and the sunny weather. But soon I couldn't see anything at all, because what I heard flooded my eyes with tears.

I didn't catch the full story, but it was about family and faith and God and hope. The voice belonged to someone who was born about the same time I was and yet whose life, in its astonishing horror and brutality, was the opposite of my own. Still, there was an instant connection, a bridge between us. She seemed to have lived out the answers to the questions nobody at my church could explain. She understood heaven and being part of God's family at a gut level. Her faith wasn't stuck as thoughts in her head. She knew the living God in her heart.

I had to track her down. I had to sit down and hear her story, one on one. I had to ask her my questions. Somehow I knew she held a piece of the puzzle of grace.

Face-to-Face with Grace

1. Have you ever felt you had to earn acceptance from another person, instead of being accepted for who you are? How did that make you feel?

2. Does God want you to be confused about your faith? Where can you go for answers?

ONE WAY
NO
CLOSED
WARNING
BEWARE OF DOG

Chapter 2
THE ORPHAN

GOD'S GRACE GOES FAR BEYOND FORGIVENESS

Stephanie Fast has never known her father. She thinks he was an American soldier — possibly an officer — who fought in the Korean conflict that started in 1950. I managed to track down Stephanie, that fleeting voice from the radio, and flew to meet her in a town house in a wooded neighborhood in the Pacific Northwest. She's small at five feet three. Her black hair falls in soft waves past her shoulders; her almond eyes are lively. Her husband Darryl, a good-natured former missionary, brought us some coffee but left us alone to chat in the living room.

Stephanie is thoughtful as she begins to answer my questions, a gentle Asian cadence in her voice. At times she looks off to the side, as if reliving the experience she's struggling to describe.[4]

"I don't know exactly when or where I was born," Stephanie says with a shrug. "Possibly, it was in Pusan, since I was told I had an accent from that region. But when? I don't know."

"My earliest memory goes back to my third birthday," I said, looking at Stephanie. "I lost a wooden sailboat that my grandparents gave me as a gift. I was crushed." I chuckled at the thought. "Such are the traumas of a middle-class kid growing up in the suburbs of Chicago. I'm sure your earliest memory is much different. What's the first thing you recall?"

She smiled and thought for a moment. "I was about the same age — three or four," she replied. "It was the harvest festival in Korea, when family members come to the ancestral home. I remember all the fun. The sweets and games and wearing a beautiful dress. But I vividly recall my mom being so sad and sorrowful."

"Do you know why?"

"Well, that night I heard arguing between family members about the choice that she had to make for her future."

Stephanie's mother had the chance to marry, but the new husband refused to take Stephanie.

"For her, the choice was, 'Do I want a future? If I do, then I can't have this child with me,'" Stephanie said. "I remember my mom crying and holding me all night."

"Was this because of discrimination against children born to parents who weren't married?"

"Yes, especially biracial ones. We were a reminder of an ugly war. When I was younger, I looked different from the other children. My hair and skin color were lighter. And I had wild, curly hair, which was quite unusual. So people knew I was a half-breed."

"How did the family drama end?"

"At some point my mother reached her decision — she would entrust me to someone else. She told me I was going to my uncle's home. Within a few days, I remember walking to the city with her. It was the first time I ever heard a train. I asked her about it, and she said to me, 'That's where we're going.'

"When the train came, she got on board with me. She gave me a cloth, about the size of a scarf, tied around a lunch and a couple of extra sets of clothing. She got on her knees and told me, 'Don't be afraid.' She said I should get off the train with the other people and my uncle would meet me. Then she left."

"What happened when you eventually got off the train?" I asked.

For a moment, Stephanie didn't answer. She slowly shook her head.

"No one came for me."

"You must have been so scared," I said.

"Not at first," Stephanie continued. "I thought, *I'll stand here on the platform, and my uncle will come for me.* But when evening came, the trains stopped. The trainmaster came out and asked me what I was doing. I told him I was waiting for my uncle. That was the first time someone called me what in English would be translated as *a piece of garbage*," she said.

"What happened next?"

"The trainmaster shooed me away. I left and found an oxen cart that was leaning against a wall. I crawled in, gathered some straw around me, opened up the cloth, and ate some food my mom had given me. I tried to go to sleep, but I remember hearing dogs, strange noises, and rustling sounds. I was scared, and yet I wasn't overly panicked."

"Even at that age?" I asked, shaking my head. I couldn't imagine someone being alone and homeless so young.

"I trusted my mom," Stephanie said. "And somewhere in my mind I thought my uncle would come for me."

I hesitated before asking my next question. Finally, I said, "As you look back, do you think there ever really was an uncle?"

She didn't flinch. "Honestly, I have no idea. It could be that my mom really was entrusting me to someone and I simply made a mistake by getting off at the wrong station. But in those days in Korea, it wasn't uncommon for mothers to abandon their children, especially if they were biracial. Sometimes they couldn't take the harassment. They often left the children in train stations or other public areas."

"So you don't really know your mother's intentions?" I asked.

Her eyes were downcast. "No, I don't," she said. Her eyes met mine again. "But I want to think the best of her. I have to. I guess all orphans think of their mother as a princess. But I was basically on my own for at least two to three years."

"How in the world did you manage to survive at age four living in the streets?"

"Only the Lord," Stephanie said. "I was already a bit self-sufficient, because my mother had always been busy in the rice fields and wasn't there to take care of me all the time. One thing about Third World children is that they sort of raise themselves. So that, in itself, was a blessing.

"The first few days or weeks, I cried for my mommy. I was always trying to find my way back to her. Maybe she would be over the next hill. Maybe she would be around the next corner. If I saw a village from the distance, I would think, *Oh, that's my village*, and I would run into it.

"But it was never my village."

LOCUSTS AND FIELD MICE

"What did you eat?" I asked Stephanie.

"Actually, food was plentiful in the country, except in the winter," she said. "I could steal whatever I wanted. There were fruit fields, vegetable fields, and rice fields. As long as I didn't get caught, I could eat.

"I remember following a group of homeless children. At night they would crawl on their bellies into the fields and get what we called sweet melons. So every night I would wait for the watchman of the field to fall asleep and I would crawl on my belly to get what I wanted to eat.

"Plus, the rice fields were full of grasshoppers and locusts. I would catch them and poke a rice straw through their heads until I had a whole string of them, which I'd tie to my belt. By the end of the day, they were pretty much dried. I'd eat them. And I killed field mice. They would come out of the same hole at the same time every day. I learned to be really, really patient. When they stuck out their heads, I would grab them quicker than they could go back down the hole. I pretty much ate everything — the skin, the ears, the tail."

"What about the winters?" I asked. "They must have been unbearable for you."

"Yes, they were very cold, and I had nowhere to go and no food. Really, I should have died that first winter. I don't know how I survived, except I remember I found a foxhole to live in. I gathered whatever straw I could find from the rice fields and brought it in to make a little den. I'd go down to the village when everybody was sleeping and steal what I could from the villagers."

"Did the villagers know you were there?"

"Oh yes. Every once in a while a kind woman would leave her kitchen door open for me. I would curl up on the dirt floor by the stove and stay warm. Those were answers to prayers, because in my den I would be shivering all night."

"You found kindness, but you also experienced a lot of horrible treatment," I said.

"Once I was caught stealing food," Stephanie said. "I remember a farmer grabbing me by the back of my neck, calling me a name and saying, 'We've got to get rid of her.' The other farmers said, 'Yeah, she's nothing but a menace. Let's tie her to the water wheel.'

"They grabbed me by my feet and shoulders, took me to the water wheel on the canal, and tied me face up. If I close my eyes, I can still tell you the cloud formations that I saw. I remember hearing myself scream. I remember my feet and my legs being stretched. I remember going under the water. I remember the pebbles and sand going into my mouth and nose. I remember coming up, spitting it all out, screaming. I could taste blood. My eyes got swollen — and then, all of a sudden the water wheel stopped.

"I felt a hand, and I heard a man's voice saying, 'Everything's okay. I'm going to take you off the water wheel. Don't fight me.' He took me down and placed me on the ground. My eyes were so swollen I could hardly see him, but I do remember that he was wearing white. A lot of grandfathers in Korea wore white outfits back then. He took a handkerchief, cleaned me up as best as he could, and gave me a drink of water.

"Then he said, 'These people want to hurt you. You need to leave, but you must live, little girl. It's very important. Listen to me – you must live.'"

FROM GARBAGE HEAP TO HOPE

Stephanie continued to struggle to survive, finally wandering into Daejeon, one of the largest cities in South Korea.

"Was living in the big city any better?" I asked.

"This young man came toward me and said, 'You're new here?' I said, 'Yes, I am.' He said, 'Do you need a place to stay?' No one had ever asked me to stay with them. I said, 'Yes, I do.' He said, 'Follow me.'

"There was a river that ran through the city, and the embankment had become a children's village. Hundreds of orphans lived on both sides. He was a leader of a little gang that oversaw everything, and he let me be a part of that gang.

The first few days were wonderful. When they got food, they shared with me. They had blankets that they shared with me. They built bonfires and told folk stories.

"But after a few days, they started picking on me and treating me really badly. I was only seven. I don't know how long I was with them, but a cholera epidemic swept through South Korea. I became very, very sick." Cholera causes people to lose a lot of weight, have a high fever, and become delirious. "I thought, *I've got to leave here. I'll go back into the country where the air is better and I can get fresh food. Everything will be okay.*

"I was walking through a dark alley and saw another child, who most likely had cholera. She was screaming. I didn't know how sick we were, but I was thinking, *She's hungry. I'm hungry, so I'll go steal some food.*

"But we were caught by farmers. They took us to a building that had been bombed out during the war and was filled with gutter rats. I was afraid of that building. It was where the rats lived, and we never went there. The farmers — there were four or five of them — threw us into that building. I can recall picking up that little girl. I remember screaming, but that's the last thing I remember."

"What's your next memory?"

"Opening my eyes and staring into blue eyes."

"Blue eyes? Whose were they?"

"Iris Eriksson, a World Vision nurse from Sweden. Her job was to rescue babies from the street, because at that time children were being abandoned left and right. Korea was still trying to survive after the war. If a family had more babies than it could feed, they just abandoned them. Miss Eriksson was told to bring back the babies — not older kids like me — because they were more likely to survive, more likely to get adopted, and less likely to have behavioral issues."

"So what happened to you?"

"Miss Eriksson found me on a garbage heap and realized I was more sick than alive. Of course, she felt pity for me, but I was much too old for her clinic. She actually got up and was going to leave me there, but she said two things happened that changed her mind. As she walked away, she said her legs felt really, really heavy. She didn't know why. As she was trying to figure it out, she heard an audible voice."

I must have looked startled, because Stephanie let out a laugh. "You had to be there when she was telling it, you know? Miss Eriksson said, 'I heard a voice in my native tongue and it only said two words: *She's mine.*' She was stunned, to say the least!"

"There was nobody around her?" I asked.

"No, not a soul," Stephanie said with a smile. "Miss Eriksson said, 'I knew it was God, and I knew I had to answer him.' So she did. She scooped me up and brought me to her clinic. She let me stay in her clinic for a few weeks. When I was healthy enough, she transferred me to the World Vision orphanage in the city."

A MAN LIKE GOLIATH

The orphanage gave Stephanie a roof over her head, but it was hardly a home. The conditions were primitive: outdoor plumbing, mats for beds, and hundreds of children needing attention.

"I was one of the oldest ones," Stephanie said. "My job became caring for the babies: washing the diapers, hanging up the diapers, folding the diapers, changing the children, putting them on my back while I was working. I loved the babies."

Love — that was a word I hadn't heard Stephanie use before. "Was love a new emotion for you ... building caring relationships with them?"

"Oh yes," she said. "When I went into the baby section, they all had their arms out, wanting me to hold them. I felt loved. The workers didn't have enough time for all of them, so I would sing to them and hug them and carry them around. Then every once in a while, a baby would disappear."

"Disappear?" I asked.

"Yes, and when I would ask where the baby went, they would say, 'He went to America.'"

"Oh, so they were adopted," I said, relieved.

"Well, that's the thing. I didn't know what adoption meant. I just knew when they said a baby went to America, it was a good thing. So one day the director said an American couple was coming to pick out a baby boy. I immediately started working to get them ready — brushing their hair, giving them baths, putting them in the best rags we had available.

"The next day, the bell rang. A worker opened the door, and it was like Mr. Goliath walked in. Not only was he tall, he was massive. Back then in Korea, the only people with extra weight were rich. I thought he must be the wealthiest person on the face of the earth. He stepped aside, and Mrs. Goliath came in. She wasn't much smaller.

"They were speaking English and had an interpreter with them. The cribs were lined up along the hallway. I watched as the man would pick up a baby and tuck it under his neck." Her face lit up at the memory.

"I was just overwhelmed by him. I don't think I had ever seen a man hold a baby like that. He brought the baby right up to his cheek, kissed him, and talked to him. It was just ... well, an emotion began to rise in me. I saw him put that baby down and pick up another baby. What I didn't realize was that I was inching closer to him. I was very curious.

"He put the second baby under his chin, and I looked into his eyes — he was crying. My heart was starting to *pump pump pump pump pump*. Something in me said, *This is good*. He put that baby down and did the same thing with a third one. But with the third one, he saw me out of the corner of his eye. Once he kissed and put the baby down, he turned around to look toward me. I started backing up, backpedaling."

"When he looked at you, what was he seeing at that time?" I asked.

"Although I was almost nine years old and had been in the orphanage for about two years, I still had dirt on my body, especially my elbows and knees. It was ground into my skin. I had lice so bad that my head was actually white. I had worms in my stomach. I had a lazy eye that sort of flopped around in its socket. My face was devoid of expression. I weighed a little less than thirty pounds. I had boils all over me and scars on my face.

"And yet still, he came over to where I was. He got down as low as he could and looked straight into my eyes. He stretched out his enormous hand and he laid it on my face, just like this," she said as she closed her eyes and tenderly demonstrated with her own hand. "His hand covered my head. Then he started stroking my face."

I sat spellbound. Here it was — the image of grace I had been seeking: A father's total acceptance of a child who has absolutely nothing to offer. Stephanie had no awards or accomplishments. She hadn't won blue ribbons in gymnastics or taken first place at piano recitals. She just had herself — weak and scarred.

"The hand on my face felt so good," Stephanie was telling me, "and inside I was saying, *Oh, keep that up! Don't let your hand go!* Nobody had ever reached out to me that way before, and I didn't know how to respond."

"What did you do?"

Her eyes widened, as if she were still astonished by her own actions. "I yanked his hand off my face," she said. "I looked him in the eye, and I spit on him! Twice, I spit on him! Then I ran away and hid in a closet."

Spit on him? My mind was reeling. Grace was throwing open a window of opportunity for her – a chance for hope, security, and a future – and she deliberately slammed it shut.

"How?" I asked. "How could you possibly do that?"

For Stephanie, this could have been the end of her story. Still, incredibly, the man and woman came back.

"I was called into the director's office the next day," Stephanie said. "There was the foreign couple. I was thinking, *I'm in real trouble now! I'm going to get punished for what I did.* But the interpreter pointed to these strangers and said, 'They want to take you to their house.'"

David and Judy Merwin, newly arrived missionaries from the United States, unexpectedly declared on that day: *This is the child we want.*

"I didn't realize that I was being adopted," Stephanie explained. "I thought I was going to become their servant. That's basically what happened in Korea. When a child got to a certain age, he or she was sold as a bond servant to rich people."

A servant. Yes, Stephanie could understand that. She could pay off the couple's kindness.

She could earn her room and board. Becoming a servant was the only way she could make any sense of her situation.

IN THE FAMILY

The Merwins had expected to adopt a boy and name him Stephen, so they gave their little girl the name Stephanie. Their house in Korea, modest by Western standards, seemed huge to her.

"I had never seen a refrigerator, a flush toilet, or a bed before. I thought, *Wow, this will be a fun place to work!* They even had eggs, which only affluent Koreans could afford. They cleaned me up, gave me antibiotics, and got me healthy. They kept feeding me, tucking me into bed, buying me new clothes, but never putting me to work."

"Did that confuse you?" I asked.

"Yes, I wondered why for several months, but I was afraid to bring it up. We'd go into a village and everybody would treat me like I was something wonderful. I couldn't understand. I had been called garbage, but now I was being treated like a princess.

"Then one day a girl said to me, 'You smell American.' I said, 'What do you mean?' She said, 'You smell like cheese.' Korean children always said foreigners smelled like cheese. I said, 'No, I'm not an American, but those Americans are really funny. They haven't put me to work yet. They are really treating me nice.'

"She looked at me with a surprised expression and said, 'Stephanie, don't you realize that you're their daughter?' That idea had never occurred to me. I said, 'No, I'm not their daughter!' And she said, 'Yes, you are! You ... are ... their ... daughter.'

"I was astonished! I turned and ran out of the room and up the hill toward my house, thinking to myself, *I'm their daughter, I'm their daughter, I'm their daughter! Oh, that's why I've been treated this way. I'm their daughter!*

"I ran into the house to my mom, who was sitting in a chair. I declared in Korean, 'I'm your daughter!' She didn't speak Korean yet, but a worker said to my mom, 'She's saying she's your daughter.' With that, big tears began to run down my mommy's face. She nodded and said to me, 'Yes, Stephanie, you're my daughter!'"

"How did that make you feel?"

Stephanie had been speaking so clearly and honestly about her life, including horrible teasing, terrible suffering, severe hunger, bitter cold, and family rejection. But now she was flustered. This time words failed her.

"It was— " she began, then threw up her hands. "There are no words, Lee. There are simply no words."

Sometimes language cannot contain grace.

"Your adoptive parents showed you so much love," I said. "Did that help you understand how much God loves you?"

"I loved the Lord as much as I knew how, but I just had so much hurt inside. My problem was that I was scared to show people my pain. If my mommy and daddy saw my pain, I thought they would bring me back to the orphanage. I was afraid they'd reject me. That went on until I was about seventeen."

"What happened then?"

"We had moved to a small town in Indiana, where my father was a pastor. I was doing everything to deny my Korean heritage. I was the only Asian in high school, and I wanted to be the perfect American girl. I was the homecoming queen and won the citizenship award. Yet every night I'd go to bed scared to death I'd lose my parents' love.

"Then the summer before my seventeenth birthday, I was sad and irritable, and my mom gently confronted me. I stalked off to my bedroom, shut the door, and looked in the mirror. I felt like

I was still nothing but a piece of trash. I crawled under the covers of my bed.

"A little while later, my dad opened the door, and I heard him call softly, 'Stephanie?' He came in and sat next to my bed and said, 'Your mother and I want you to know that we love you very much, but you seem to have a hard time accepting that love.'

"Now, I was a pastor's daughter, so I knew the Bible, right? But my dad knew better. He said, 'Stephanie, can I share with you about Jesus?' I sort of rolled my eyes and said, 'Sure.' He told me to think about Jesus — only he knew how I felt and he was the only one who could help me. Then my daddy left me by myself.

"Until that moment, I only saw Jesus as the Son of God. I knew he had come down to earth. But that night, for the first time, it dawned on me: *He understands me*. He walked in my shoes! His daddy — his earthly father — wasn't his real daddy. He slept in the straw as a child. He was ridiculed and abused. People chased him and tried to kill him ... just like they'd done to me.

"So after my dad left that night, I prayed — but my prayer was not a nice prayer. I said 'God, if you're what mom and dad say you are, then do something and do it right now!' And he did."

"What did he do?" I said.

"I started crying." Stephanie smiled. "I hadn't cried in years. I hadn't been able to. In the process of being abused and taunted, I realized that the more I cried, the more pain I would experience. That night something cold and hard broke inside of me — a wall between me and God. I couldn't stop my tears.

"I started wailing. My mom and dad came into the room. They didn't say anything. I wouldn't let them snuggle with me, so my dad held my feet and my mom held my hands, and they prayed silently to the Lord.

"Suddenly, it just came to me: Jesus knows me — *and he still loves me!* He knows all my shame, he knows all my guilt, he knows all my fears, he knows all my loneliness — yet he still loves me. I've never been the same since.

"The fact that I could finally look in the mirror and love myself was nothing less than a miracle. It's God's grace."

ADOPTED BY GOD

As I flew back home the next day, I felt like I had looked into the eyes of grace. As a child, Stephanie only experienced the worst from people. Then her life was transformed — first by an earthly father who sacrificed his dream of a son to reach out to a social outcast. Then because of a heavenly Father who sacrificed his own Son so Stephanie could experience his healing love and grace.

Stephanie went from an uncertain and insecure orphan to a securely loved child of God.

That's when it crystallized for me. God's grace not only erases the sins for which I deserved punishment, but when I believe in him, he also becomes my loving and compassionate Father.

God could have forgiven our sins and yet kept us at arm's length. He could have made us mere servants in his kingdom — and even that would have been more than we deserved. But his grace is far more outrageous than that. The Bible tells us, "Yet to all who did receive him, to those who believed in his name, he gave the right to become children of God" (John 1:12).

Children of God. Yes, I have long understood that God's grace invites us into his family. But after talking with Stephanie, I can imagine her running with joy toward home, declaring, *I'm their daughter, I'm their daughter, I'm their daughter!* What an amazing truth! I'm beyond forgiven. I'm more than a servant. I'm adopted by a Father whose love is perfect, whose approval is unconditional, whose love is never ending, and whose kindness is unlimited. A Father who is *for* me — forever. A Father who has his arms open wide as I run toward him declaring, *I'm his son!*

Face-to-Face with Grace

1. Read Hebrews 4:15–16. How do these verses show that God understands what you're going through? What do you learn from these verses about grace?

2. Do you know what it feels like to be adopted into God's family? If you've prayed to accept Jesus as your Savior, write down the feelings you had when you first made that decision.

Chapter 3
THE PRODIGAL

THE GATEWAY TO GRACE IS REPENTANCE

As broken and dangerous as Stephanie's growing up years were, Andrew Palau's were the exact opposite.

Andrew has a world-famous father who has always loved and supported him. Luis Palau, a popular evangelist whose Christian festivals, books, and radio programs have reached a billion people in seventy-five countries,[5] encouraged all four of his sons to live for the Lord. But Andrew wasn't listening.

Though Andrew put on a Christian front as a kid, he didn't live out his faith. He ignored his father's pleadings about Jesus, choosing instead to do whatever made him feel good at the time. He fell into drinking and smoking marijuana. He was kicked out of a top Christian university. He wandered purposelessly without following through on his responsibilities. At any of those times, it would have been easy to give up on him.

But Luis kept praying for him.

EVERY DECISION A BAD ONE

"I was a fool," Andrew said to me as we talked in a sparsely furnished room at Luis Palau's ministry in Portland, Oregon. "Proverbs has a lot to say about foolish people. Just go down the list — that was me."

The six-dozen references in the Old Testament book of Proverbs paint a miserable and wretched picture. Fools hate wisdom, are lazy, bring grief to their parents, lack common sense, try to trick people, think it's cool to do dangerous things, are full of pride, lie all the time, don't ask for forgiveness, refuse to pay for their mistakes, avoid discipline, and don't listen to advice.[6] And that's just the start!

"There's some pretty harsh stuff in there," I said.

"No, seriously, I was the fool of Proverbs," Andrew insisted. "I squandered every opportunity. I stumbled through life drunk or on drugs or both. Just about every decision I made was wrong. Everything was about *me* having fun, partying with friends, getting into trouble. It was a competition to see who could do the craziest stuff and laugh about it the next day. If that's not being a fool, then I don't know what is."

I was taken aback by his blunt assessment of himself — which, frankly, sounded a lot like me in my teen years. "What was driving you?" I asked. "Did you see hypocrisy in your home? Was your father not there for you?"

"No, nothing like that. I can't blame anyone else. You see, I was in love with Andrew. I wanted to be cool, so I'd be accepted by all the girls and the right guys in the right cliques. I was selfish, self-centered, self-indulgent. I was rebellious, although not because I was angry at God."

"Did you think Christianity was true?"

"Well, this is embarrassing, but I thought it probably *was* true. The thing is, I just didn't care. I loved my sin too much."

"You must have done a good job of hiding it from your parents," I said.

"Yeah, I would act like I was friendly and positive. I would say all the right things. When I had to, I'd lie to get myself out of trouble. In fact, I did everything a good evangelist's boy was supposed to do: I was part of the church's youth group, I memorized Bible verses, I went to missions conferences, and I attended church every Sunday."

Many of his party friends also attended church. So they'd act one way on Sunday and another way during the rest of the week.

"Did you ever get caught doing something bad?" I asked.

"Once in high school we were drinking, and I crashed the car in someone's front yard. We all ran away. The police found me, and I got a ticket for hit-and-run driving. Usually, I would weasel my way out of trouble. I really hated to get caught. But every time I got away with something, it made me even bolder the next time."

After high school, Andrew went to Biola University, a Christian college in Southern

GOD'S NEAT, LET'S EAT

Have you ever wondered why the prayer you say before eating is called *grace*? That's a great question! The Bible is full of examples of people praying to thank God for providing food, even Jesus and the apostle Paul did it. A longtime Jewish tradition encourages people to say a prayer of gratitude for God's provision *after* meals. The term *grace* probably developed in the early church and came from the Latin word *gratias*, which means thanks.[7]

By the way, saying "Rub-a-dub-dub. Thanks for the grub," is *not* a great way to show God your thanks.

California. But after a year of partying and drinking, the college asked him to leave because of his behavior. He changed to the University of Oregon in Eugene.

"By then, I was really out of control," Andrew said. "Nobody was looking over my shoulder, so I pushed the limits. I was still unsure of my personal identity. I'd worn so many masks for so long that when I looked in the mirror, I didn't recognize who was looking back."

Eventually, he dropped out of college, traveled to Europe, and got a job in a furniture store.

A LETTER FROM A FATHER

"My life was headed nowhere," Andrew said. "But my dad never stopped pursuing me. When I was young, he would take me for walks and tell me about Jesus. Wherever I moved, he would have his friends take me to dinner and share Christ with me. He would also write me letters."

Andrew slipped on some glasses and picked up a copy of his book *The Secret Life of a Fool*, in which he tells his story. "I especially remember a letter he wrote before he visited me in Northern Ireland," he said. "It really shows his heart."

He flipped to the right page and read parts of the letter to me. Sometimes his voice choked with emotion:

> Dear Andrew,
>
> There's a phrase that keeps coming back to me every time I pray for you and think about you

(and I do that very much as you can imagine — you are a son I love very much). When I was twenty-one, like you, I took this little phrase for myself: 'But you, man of God ...' (1 Timothy 6:11).

You were born, Andrew, to be a man of God. That's what God has for you. That is God's purpose for your life.... The Lord God loves you with an everlasting love. The first step he has taken to bring you to himself is that he went willingly and personally for you to a cross. On that cross he became your substitute. He took your place and your punishment and forever removed your guilt.

I pray first of all, Andrew, that you would open your heart to Jesus Christ. The day I prayed and asked Christ to give me eternal life, a counselor used Romans 10:9–10 with me. He personalized it just for me. I've never asked you, Andrew: Have you ever asked him personally?

If you confess with your lips, Andrew, that Jesus is Lord and believe in your heart, Andrew, that God raised Jesus from the dead, you, Andrew, shall be saved. For it is with your heart, Andrew, that you believe and are justified and it is with your mouth that you confess, Andrew, and are saved. Then verse 13 — "For everyone who calls on the name of the Lord will be saved."

If you haven't made that decision, Andrew, and if you want me to help pray with you — and nothing would give me greater joy in the whole world — I would do it ... if you want.

"Follow me, and I will make you fishers of men."[8] I took that quote from Jesus very seriously at your age. I love it. It's the best life in the world. You will enjoy it too, my son, if you follow Jesus with all your heart and soul. What else is there in this rebellious world? Not much.

See you soon. I love you and pray for you, Dad.[9]

Andrew let the word *Dad* linger for a few moments, then closed the book, set it on the desk, and slipped his glasses into a shirt pocket.

"That's my father," he said finally. "The same things he said to 100,000 people, he said to his son. He knew that the only thing that could change my life would be God's grace. He saw that so clearly, but I was so blind to it. His confidence has always been in the power of the gospel."

Fast-forward a few years from when his dad wrote that letter. By now Andrew was living in Boston, starting on the bottom rung of the corporate ladder at a clothing retailer. With little money, he lived in a cramped apartment. He remained as far from God as ever.

Luis waited until the winter temperatures in Boston were unbearably cold, and then called to invite Andrew to one of his evangelistic rallies. When Andrew insisted he wasn't interested, Luis casually let it be known that the event would be in Jamaica. That meant marlin fishing. Andrew started to pack his bags.

Andrew stayed with a Jamaican businessman and his family, which included their son Chris and daughter Wendy. As Andrew hung around with them and their friends, he was amazed—and intrigued—by their fresh and enthusiastic faith, which seemed to reflect the "abundant life" he had always heard his parents talk about.[10]

"They were fun and normal, warm and friendly, engaged with the community, and they were sold out to Christ in a very radical way," Andrew recalled. "Jesus seemed so real and present to them. I listened as they told others about how God had healed their addictions and restored their relationships. I was thinking, *This is what I need! I can't keep pretending that my shame and guilt aren't dogging me. Something has got to happen.*"

On three of the five nights when Luis preached at the 35,000-seat Kingston National Stadium, Andrew attended with his new friends.

"I always respected Dad and the sincerity of his message," Andrew told me. "On the last night of the crusade, I went with a receptive attitude. I really wanted to hear the voice of the God who had so completely changed the lives of these new friends of mine."

"And did you?" I asked.

"Well, as I sat there and listened, it struck me that Dad's message was different than before. It was like he was picking on me. He really went after me. And then I realized: This was the same message he almost always gives. He was talking about the story of the rich young ruler — only, I wasn't rich and I ruled nothing.[11] It had nothing to do with me, and yet the Lord was pressing me.

"When Dad gave the invitation to receive Christ, I found myself saying in my spirit, *Lord, this is what I want. Please come into my life. I'm going a new direction. I want heaven, and I want to do the right thing. Everything I say I want to do but can't seem to do — I want to do it.* At that moment, I determined to stop drinking, break off my inappropriate relationships, and start going to church."

"Were you sincere?" I said.

"Yes, it was very genuine," Andrew replied. "I wanted what God was offering. I realized it was so much better than the empty life I had been leading."

Luis typically ends his rallies with a call for

people to come forward if they want to follow Christ.

"Did you respond to the call to go forward?" I asked.

"I felt compelled to go, but I resisted it," Andrew said. "A lot of people did walk forward, though, and many of them were sobbing. Afterward I felt a sense of relief. I immediately told Wendy, and she was thrilled. She said I needed to tell my parents."

"How did you feel about doing that?" I said.

"I was hesitant, honestly. As my dad remembers it, I bounded into their hotel room and declared, 'I did it! I did it! I've become a Christian!' As I recall, though, the conversation felt awkward."

"In what way?"

"I told them about my decision and, of course, they were very encouraging and affirming," Andrew said. "They'd seen this kind of response in people at a lot of their crusades over the years. They knew that what God started, he would somehow complete.[12] But there was also a little bit of a 'wait-and-see attitude.'"

"Hmmm. Was it warranted?"

"Well," he replied, "based on what happened next, it was pretty discerning on their part."

BACKSLIDING BACK TO THE BEACH

Andrew's friends in Boston were astonished—and skeptical—when he told them he was now a Christian. They watched warily as he went to church and started to clean up his life. But the "new Andrew" lasted only a month.

"One night I went out with some friends to a bar—not to drink, but just to hang out with them," Andrew said to me. "Pretty soon I had a beer. Then another. Then six, plus three straight shots of alcohol. I started smoking dope. Before long, I was involved again with some of the girls I knew I should be avoiding."

"So everything fell apart?" I asked.

"Completely. I embarrassed myself—and the Lord. My friends were laughing at me. I was ashamed and humiliated. My life started to spiral downward again. I kept thinking, *How could my commitment to God have been so real to me, and now this? How could I have been so sincere and yet fail so badly? What am I supposed to do now?*"

"Looking back, what do you think caused you to backslide?" I asked.

"It turns out I had more in common with the rich young ruler than I thought. Jesus challenged him to give himself wholly to God, but he wouldn't give up his wealth. He insisted on clinging to it, even if it meant walking away from Jesus. Well, I had built my own kingdom of pleasure, where I reigned supreme. I didn't really want God to rule all of my life. I wanted to hang on to the partying stuff."

"Still," I said, "the prayer in Jamaica was a step in the right direction."

"Yeah, it was a step," Andrew said. "My heart seemed to be opening to God. But as I look back at it, my prayer in Jamaica was hollow. A salvation prayer doesn't mean much unless you authentically turn from sin and allow God to take over your life. *That's* what he deserves. I was saying, *I want all the good things you offer — the forgiveness, the release from guilt, heaven, and all that — and I'll try my hardest to do good to keep you happy. Yes, I want you, God, but without giving up* Me. *Is it a deal?*"

Shaking his head, Andrew said: "God doesn't bargain like that. Not at all. He doesn't want part of our lives. He wants all of us, because he gave everything, including his Son, for us."

A few months later Andrew went back to Jamaica to visit Wendy. He had been captivated by her charm and intrigued by her deep faith in Christ. When Andrew got together with her and her friends again, he tried his best to act like a Christian. It didn't take them long to see through his charade.

Andrew was busted. They had figured out that he wasn't following Jesus. So he admitted that he was struggling spiritually and had botched his efforts to lead a better life.

"One of the guys named Steve invited me to pray and read the Bible with him the next morning," Andrew said.

On their knees at dawn, Steve read the opening verses of Romans 12: "Therefore, I urge you, brothers and sisters, in view of God's mercy, to offer your bodies as a living sacrifice, holy and pleasing to God — this is your true and proper worship. Do not conform to the pattern of this world, but be transformed by the renewing of your mind. Then you will be able to test and approve what God's will is — his good, pleasing and perfect will."[13]

As they began to discuss this passage, Andrew started to weep out of frustration. He had heard the words, but their meaning eluded him.

"My comprehension level was zero," he said to me. "I had studied English literature in college and grown up in a Christian home. I knew how to dig into the meaning of a text. But I was blind when it came to the Bible. I had absolutely no idea what this passage meant. I really wanted to hear from God through his Word, but it was like there was a wall between me and the verses."

Seeing Andrew's frustration, Steve offered a solution: "You need to come up to the mountain."

Every year a group of Christians went on a retreat to the tropical Blue Mountains outside Kingston for a few days of friendship building, prayer, worship, and teaching from the Bible. Andrew felt drawn to go, so he made some last-minute changes to his plans. Silently, he prayed: *Lord, I'm open. Let's face it: I've opened myself up to all the garbage of the world — why wouldn't I open myself up to whatever you have for me?*

CONFESSION AND CLEANSING

At the two-day gathering, the teaching focused on big and important ideas: the greatness and power of God, the authority of God, God's holiness, and the biblical picture of God as Creator and King of the universe. They talked about the Holy Spirit's work in the world, convicting people of sin, drawing them to God's kingdom, and changing them from the inside.

More and more, Andrew wanted to personally and intimately experience this awesome

God. *What's it going to take?* he kept asking God. *If you're real — if all this is true — then I have to know for sure.*

He began begging God for a supernatural encounter. *Lord, just do this one more thing: Reveal yourself to me. Stand before me, and I'll know you're real. You can do that, for sure. You've got the power. Then I'll believe.*

Over and over, he implored God to appear. Despite Andrew's pleas … nothing.

Frustrated and downcast, almost as a last ditch effort, Andrew changed his prayer. *God,* he whispered, *what is keeping me from you?*

Instantly, he was startled by a distinct response he felt in his spirit. *Do you really want to know, Andrew?* Now he was even more eager: Here was the personal engagement with God he had been so earnestly seeking.

Andrew's eyebrows rose as he described to me what happened next. His words came tumbling out, his tone a mix of astonishment and wonder — and horror.

"In a flash, God miraculously opened my eyes to what had been keeping us apart: There before me was all the garbage of my life, all of my lying, cheating, stealing, and abusive relationships, all the pride, all the addictions and people I had hurt, all the deception and hypocrisy and callousness. I saw it all, this seemingly insurmountable pile of sin stacked as high as I could see.

"I was horrified. I gasped and fell on my face, embarrassed and humiliated and remorseful, bawling like I never had before. I was heaving with sobs. My tears fell on the floor. *God,* I said, *how could I have been such a fool? Please forgive me! Please take this away! I can't live with it anymore. What hope do I have when all of this garbage is in me?*

"God's response in that moment was right out of Scripture: *If you confess your sin, Andrew, I am able to forgive you of your unrighteousness. I will clean it out. I will take it as far as the east is from the west. I will remember your sin no more.*[14]

"I started confessing as fast as God could bring my sins into my mind. One after the other, and I would cry out for forgiveness and he would release them. By his grace, God was also piecing me back together.

"So there I was, facedown on the floor, and some of the guys came over and put their arms on my shoulder and said, 'This is your time, Andrew. Make sure you get it all out. Don't try to hide anything from the Lord.' They brought me to a room and helped me verbalize some of my confession.

"After two or three hours, it was over. It was like God had flipped on a light in my soul. I felt such incredible relief — an utter sense of release from all the things that had trapped me. For the first time, I understood what Jesus meant when he said he will not only make us free, but *free indeed.*[15] Like a captive not only released from prison, but running into the arms of his father. I looked out at the mountain and it was as if the whole world was fresh and new — beautiful, just beautiful.

"I kept thanking God for his grace and then, out of sheer gratitude, I whispered, 'I will tell everyone what you have done.' As the words left me, he replied, *You will.* Not in the form of a question, but more of a statement, like he was sealing his calling on my life."

THE PRODIGAL'S ONLY WAY

This time things went differently when he told his father. "I came down the mountain and called my dad immediately," Andrew told me. "I said, 'You'll never guess what happened.' I described what God had done and he said, 'Oh, wow, Andrew, *that's* what we've been waiting for.'"

"Repentance," I said.

"Exactly." Andrew nodded. "I needed to confess that I'm wrong and God is right. I needed to see my sinfulness in contrast with his holiness. I needed his cleansing and leadership of my life. *This* is how transformation begins. It's not enough just to pray, *God, make me a better person.* It was repentance that opened the floodgates of grace for me – and it was grace that changed my life and eternity."

Years after his soul-healing experience with God in Jamaica, Andrew joined his dad's ministry. He carried his father's bags for four years and then spent six years living in various cities to serve local churches and come up with music and sports festivals where his dad would share the gospel.

In the years since then, Andrew has become an evangelist himself, telling the story of God's grace to crowds of tens of thousands of people and to individual inmates in prison.[16]

Oh, and remember Wendy? She and Andrew have now been married for more than twenty years. The prodigal came home and found a loving heavenly Father, a loving earthly father, and a loving wife. God doesn't just sprinkle us with grace, he sends a tidal wave that overwhelms and changes our lives forever.

Face-to-Face with Grace

1. Have you ever made a foolish decision? What did you do to change your ways?

2. Read 1 John 1:9. Have you ever confessed your deepest, darkest secrets to God? If not, what's stopping you?

BANG!

Chapter 4 THE PROFESSOR

GOD'S GRACE IS LIKE NOTHING ELSE IN THE WORLD

Craig Hazen has always been a good guy. Smart, well-mannered, friendly, witty. He was a favorite of his teachers in high school because he actually *liked* to learn. The honor roll? That was no problem. When he walked into the library, he felt like he was on a treasure hunt.

Craig was a science geek, working after school as an assistant to a physician and planning a career in medical research. Sure, he was mischievous, once instigating an enormous donut fight that's still talked about today at his former school.

Because he was a nice guy, Craig felt like he didn't need God. As a teenager, he believed science — not Christianity — held the keys to understanding the big issues of life.

FROM EXPERIMENT TO LIFESTYLE

Some people are in obvious need of God's forgiveness — like the brutal slave trader John Newton, who ended up so amazed by grace that he penned the classic hymn "Amazing Grace." Then there's Saul of Tarsus, who killed Christians before celebrating grace after he met the risen Lord and became the apostle Paul. But then there are the Craig Hazens of the world — the nice guys who always seem to walk a moral path.

"How did you come to the point of recognizing your need for grace?" I asked Craig in his book-lined office in La Mirada, California, just

SAYING GRACE

Does your family say grace before meals? About half of all families in the United States pray before they eat at least one time every day.[17]

off the campus of Biola University. The same school that booted out Andrew Palau had invited Craig in as one of its top professors.

"When I was a senior in high school, I was a smart kid," he answered. "Everyone thought I was going somewhere. No Christian had ever offered me good reasons to believe, so I came to the conclusion that the world was probably all about me."

Still, there was that chemistry teacher, the one who kept putting posters about God on her classroom walls. She had an undeniable sense of peace that intrigued him. Then there was the cute girl who invited him to church one night.

He stopped and smiled before continuing. "This girl invited me to hear an evangelist at a church. I remember the message was based on the fourth chapter of John, where Jesus offers the Samaritan woman 'living water' that leads to eternal life.[18] I figured, *What do I have to lose?* I walked forward at the altar call, but frankly it was just an experiment at the time."

"An experiment?" I asked.

"Yeah," Craig said. "I wanted to see what would happen."

"So what happened?"

"They took me to a side room for counseling," Craig said. "Before long, all the counselors were clustered around me, because I was peppering them with questions that nobody could answer."

"So you walked out that night unconvinced?" I said.

"Pretty much, but I had started a journey. They began giving me books and tapes and following up with phone calls. I studied the issues for several months and finally God sealed it. I became convinced Christianity is true.

"At that point I began to understand why I had been attracted to the peace that I had seen in my chemistry teacher — the one who kept putting God posters on the walls. Even though I was a good kid, I was still a sinner. I was experiencing a sense of anxiety and alienation that I couldn't quite put my finger on. God began to deal with that in my life.

"In fact," he continued, "here's a funny thing about grace. A couple of years later, evangelists came to the college I was attending and brought some guys who had very dramatic testimonies. They stood on the cement planter in the quad and told about how they had been in the gutter and did all kinds of horrible things, yet the Lord found them and lifted them up. And I was thinking, *Man, I want to jump up there too and give a different testimony*. You see, I *wasn't* in the gutter. I *wasn't* the dreg of society. I had great promise. Everybody thought I was on the road to success. And guess what? I still desperately needed God!

"Here's what I came to understand: having good table manners, getting As in school, saying 'please' and 'thank you,' and being nice to people — that's all pretty trivial stuff. Actually, I was in rebellion against a Holy God so powerful that he could speak billions of galaxies into existence. I was ignoring him. My sins — my pride, my smugness, my selfishness, and all of my secret deceit — had created an enormous gap between me and God.

"That's what sin does. It fosters a sense of separation and being unfulfilled. God is perfect. He is holy and pure. And I certainly wasn't, neither in my thoughts or actions. The Bible stresses that nobody is truly good — Romans 3:23 says, 'All have sinned and fall short of the glory of God.' Over time, I came to realize that the plain language of that verse means what it explicitly says. '*All* have sinned,' and that includes me.

"I needed forgiveness, and I found grace through Jesus."

Three-and-a-half decades after walking into that church, Craig has earned his doctorate in religious studies. He's written numerous books and articles explaining and defending the Christian faith and is considered one of the top experts on world religions.

Craig was the ideal person to talk to about two issues I wanted to explore.

First, what about the good person who helps old ladies across the street, doesn't kick puppies, and always plays by the rules? Usually, the stories we hear about God's grace are from gang-members-turned-gospel-singers or drug addicts who now get their highs from Jesus. These astonishing tales of radical transformation show up all the time in Christian TV shows, magazines, and books. As inspiring as those accounts may be, what about the vast numbers of people, like Craig, who succeed in having decent lives? Do they *really* need God's grace?

Second, what about the billions of people around the planet who follow other religions? Is grace a universal part of faith that's found in every religion or is this concept exclusive to Christianity?

BEYOND MERCY TO GRACE

"Mercy and compassion — they pop up in virtually every religious tradition," Craig said after I introduced my questions. "But it's important to understand that the biblical concept of grace goes much further than that. In Christianity, God isn't just saying, 'I'm not going to punish you for what you've done.' That would be merciful, but he takes a dramatic next step by giving us something glorious — complete forgiveness and eternal life as a pure gift.

"It's like parents who catch their kids doing something wrong and they don't just let them off the hook, but they give them ice cream as well, because they love them so much," he said, flashing a smile. "That's what grace is — an amazing gift that we don't deserve. It's extravagant. It's unmerited favor that God bestows freely to those willing to receive it. We can't earn it. We can't contribute to it. We can't repay him for it.

We can't take any credit for it. But God offers it, because he made us in his image, and he wants to have a relationship with us for eternity. That's the good news of the gospel. But to fully grasp it, we have to understand the bad news as well."

"By 'bad news,' you mean sin, right?" I asked.

"That's right," Craig replied. "You can't really have a good concept of grace unless you really understand sin."

"And that," I said, "is a problem these days. Many people have lost the concept of sin."

"Yes, in Christianity, sin creates a gap between us and God that is simply insurmountable. Trying to cross it is like jumping off the Newport Beach pier [in California] and trying to land in Hawaii," he said, gesturing toward the Pacific Ocean.

"The first time, you don't get very far, so you train harder and harder," he continued. "You work with the best long jumpers in the world. You buy new athletic shoes. You lift weights and eat your spinach. And the next time you manage to jump twelve inches farther. Good for you. But the gap is still nearly 2,500 miles! To overcome a divide that wide takes an almighty and all-loving God to provide a bridge, which our heavenly Father does through the cross of Christ. People don't understand that in our culture."

"People don't see themselves as being very bad and therefore they don't appreciate the magnitude of this gift of grace that God is offering," I said. "Is that what you're saying?"

"Yeah, that's *the* disease today. We've lost an understanding of the holiness of God," he replied. "Remember when Peter first met Jesus? Peter declared, 'Don't even gaze on me; I'm a sinful man!'[19] I don't think he had any idea that this was the Son of God standing before him. He merely sensed that here was holiness, and he instantly understood that he was a wretched individual. Today people think, *I'm no mass murderer; therefore, I'm wonderful!*

"We've lost sight of the holiness of God and the depth of our own sin — and those are tough things to communicate to our culture. But the truth is if you've ever lied, you're a liar. If you've ever stolen anything, you're a thief. When we start thinking of it that way, we begin to see our own sinfulness."

POSTER BOY FOR GRACE

I pointed to the Bible on the table between us. "Which of Jesus' teachings best explains grace for you?"

"It's got to be the story of the Prodigal Son,"[20] Craig quickly said. "It's over the top! In this parable, the younger son takes his inheritance and says, 'I'm going my own way.' The father probably took a deep breath and said, 'Oh, I hope one day he comes back!' And after a disastrous life that helps the son realize the enormity of his sin, he *does* come back. But before he gets home, the father sees him and without a moment of hesitation runs to him with a ring, sandals, and a feast. The father doesn't just begrudgingly allow his son secondary status as a disfavored servant, but he orders a party in his honor and reinstates him as his child."

Craig's eyebrows shot up. "Wow!" he exclaimed. "What a story of undeserved favor! You don't find anything like that in the other religions of the world."

"Are you sure?" I asked. "I thought there was a story in Buddhist literature that's like the prodigal son parable."

"Well, they're similar to the degree that they both involve sons who rebelled, left home, saw the error of their ways, and came back home. But the Buddhist story ends quite differently — the son has to work off his misdeeds."

"How?" I said.

"He ends up toiling for twenty-five years, hauling animal dung. That's a stark contrast between the God of grace and a religion where people have to work their way to favor."[21]

My hand swept toward the array of books on Craig's shelves. "You've spent your academic life studying the religions of the world. Are you saying that grace can't be found anywhere else?"

"The Christian view of grace sets it apart from all the other great religions; there's no question about it," he said. "In the end, Christianity's teachings on grace are unparalleled in world religions. In short, the Prodigal Son is still the poster boy for grace."

A FAITH THAT CAN BE TESTED

"How does a transformed life help support the truth of Christianity?" I asked. "Or does it?"

"On the one hand," Craig replied, "I've seen examples of people who have been so dramatically changed that I can only attribute it to the work of Christ. So, yes, I believe that a Christian's testimony about the power of God in his life can be persuasive to a degree. But it needs to be combined with other evidence to really make the case for Christianity.

"On the other hand, it's true that people in other religious movements can have wonderful experiences that make them feel spiritually uplifted. In fact, good feelings can be generated in so many different ways that we ought not let our feelings dictate which religious direction we're going to go.

"Yes, you want to be transformed by your faith, but you also want to know that it's the real deal. So while grace sets apart Christianity, so does truth. Jesus was filled with grace *and* truth. In Christianity you can *know* the truth, not just through some sort of spiritual experience, but also through careful investigation. Defenders of the Christian faith carefully examine historical documents and archeological evidence. Christianity can be tested. When you check it out, you find that it's supported by philosophy, science, and history.

"So Christianity is different," Craig continued. "First, because of grace. Second, because it's testable. And third, because it paints a picture that matches the way the world is in a way that other religions don't. We are called as Christians to help people who are suffering, not dismiss their suffering as an illusion and thereby minimize or dismiss it.

"What I'm saying is this: Christianity — in so many key areas — reflects reality in a way that other faiths simply do not."

Our discussion prompted a verse to jump into my mind: "For the law was given through Moses; grace and truth came through Jesus Christ."[22] As Craig said, both grace and truth are important. *Grace* opens the door to a relationship with God through no merit of our own. Yet our faith is merely wishful thinking unless Christianity is based on *truth*. It is a testable faith.

My cell phone buzzed, signaling my need to end our conversation. I packed up my recording gear and thanked Craig for his time.

"Honestly," he said with a boyish smile, "there's nothing I enjoy discussing more than grace. It's an inexhaustible topic."

As I drove through the snarled roadways of Southern California, I was amazed by the number of church buildings I saw, both old-fashioned and modern. Some had crosses on top that rose toward the sky. To me, each cross served not just as a reminder of the grace God freely gives us, but so much more. It was a symbol of what Christ had to do for us to receive that grace and how important it is for us to share that truth with the world.

Face-to-Face with Grace

1. What is it about grace that sets Christianity apart from other religions?

2. How deeply have you looked at your faith in Jesus Christ? What could you do to gain a deeper understanding and commitment?

Chapter 5
THE EVANGELIST

LIVING EVERY DAY UNDER GOD'S GRACE

Brandon Rys began life pretty normally. His father would say Brandon was better than normal because he was good at everything he did. He taught himself how to read at age three and learned how to ride a bicycle without training wheels in no time. Rollerblading, baseball, soccer — name a sport and Brandon would try it. He was diagnosed with asthma at an early age, so he always had an inhaler close by, but he'd do anything, even waterskiing.

Soon his family realized that Brandon's life would be anything but normal according to most definitions. At first doctors thought he had cystic fibrosis, because he was so sick and had a lot of congestion in his lungs. But when he was five, he reached down to pet his dog … and broke his back. Then everybody knew his condition was much more serious.

Brandon started spending as much time in hospitals as he did at home. The diagnoses started adding up. His medical chart reads like an encyclopedia of sicknesses. He has primary immune deficiency, osteoporosis, arthritis, adrenal insufficiency, seizure disorder, glaucoma, cataracts, asthma — and the list goes on and on. While some of these conditions aren't life threatening, the combination makes daily life pretty difficult.

Basically, his immune system, which is supposed to attack diseases, is attacking the rest of Brandon's body. Some days it attacks his brain, causing seizures. Other days it attacks somewhere else. And with the severe osteoporosis, his bones are as brittle as an eighty-year-old's.

To combat this onslaught of disease, Brandon takes an arsenal of medications — more than twenty a day — through a port in his stomach. Every month, he has to drive over 400 miles for special intravenous treatments. He's on a first-name basis with many doctors and nurses.

Every day Brandon lives in pain. Yet the first thing you notice when you meet Brandon is his smile. He doesn't constantly smile, but when he does, it's genuine and easy.

Once he was asked to share his thoughts on "Why Children Get Sick" in a newsletter that's sent around the world. He wrote that everything happens to the glory of God: Children are better able to be happy in their circumstances. Plus, they don't blame anybody and are quick to trust God.

"I write this as a child who has been ill his whole life," Brandon put in the newsletter. "Yet I have the greatest joy in knowing Jesus."

When I learned Brandon often spent part of his summer in Colorado, I knew I had to hear his story to better put together this puzzle of grace. I'd long understood that God gives us the grace to live each day. God's grace helps us deal with the occasional struggles we encounter. But what if every day was a struggle? What would God's grace look like then?

I asked my friend, Jesse Florea, to fill me in about Brandon. Jesse drove from his house in Colorado Springs to Wind River Ranch. This Christian dude ranch sits in the heart of the Rocky Mountains, just outside Estes Park. As he pulled up the long dirt road, Jesse told me that a yeehawing cowgirl ran out to greet him. She took him to a cabin, so he could meet Brandon and his parents. Brandon stood to say hello. Dressed in a cowboy hat, this Texas native seemed at ease surrounded by horses and at 9,200 feet of elevation above sea level.

He quickly sat back down on a sofa. Standing wasn't easy for him after a stroke-like syndrome in his brain compromised his balance. He usually uses a walker because of his balance issues and limited eyesight from the glaucoma.

As Jesse started the interview, Brandon's parents sat in the background. Mature beyond his twelve years, Brandon answered each question honestly and thoroughly ... and sometimes with a little mischievous humor.

Here's how his interview went[23]:

"So what's a normal day look like for you?" I (Jesse) asked.

"I wake up," Brandon said. "My mom pulls open my eyelids because, basically, that's the only way I can wake up. I get up, go to the bathroom, and do my inhalers. Maybe listen to Adventures in Odyssey CDs. I brush my teeth. If it's Sunday, we go to church. But if it's any other day, I do school. The average is an hour and a half for school. Then I eat lunch, go to physical therapy, come home, and take a nap. When I wake up, we eat dinner. Listen to some more Adventures in Odyssey. Take my other meds and go to bed."

"So your main medications are inhalers a couple of times a day?"

"Those are the main medications that I do," Brandon explained. "I have about twenty more that my mom gives me."

"Most kids just want a normal life. Do you feel normal?" I asked.

"My definition of normal used to be never being in a hospital, getting to do whatever I wanted, whenever I wanted," Brandon said. "Jump, play, ride my bike, go on sleepovers. Now I understand that normal isn't like that. Normal is how God made you. He made each person special, and that's normal."

"A lot of kids don't like how God made them," I said. "There are things they'd want to change. But you've learned to accept exactly who you are at a young age, and God's given you many opportunities to do different things. Do you feel special in those ways?"

"I've been on a Southwest Airlines TV commercial, spoken for the Make-A-Wish Foundation and Ronald McDonald House. I've met former President George W. Bush. But I don't really think of myself. I just want to get the message across to people that God loves them and that Jesus died for their sins and rose again. If you believe in him, you can live with him forever."

NOT ASHAMED OF THE GOSPEL

The more he talked, the stronger Brandon's voice seemed to get. And when he started talking about telling other people about Jesus, he leaned forward with excitement.

"What are some ways that you've been outspoken for Christ?" I asked.

"I've been in the hospital quite a few times," Brandon answered. "Most of the doctors and nurses aren't Christians. Once when I was stuck in the hospital, one of my nurses came in. He was a man. He saw my dinosaur slippers and asked, 'How do you think the dinosaurs died?' So I told him the story about the flood and how God wouldn't accept anybody into heaven who had sinned. Then he said, 'You think I'm probably going to hell.' And I said, 'Well, yes, but you don't have to.' And it gave me an opportunity to spread the gospel that way.

"And when I met President Bush, newspapers at home wanted to know about it. So at the end of the conversation, the newspaper lady asked 'Oh, do you think that President Bush is strong in his faith? How do you feel about your faith?' So I gave her the whole gospel."

Brandon's mother smiled over her son's shoulder, and I made eye contact with her.

"The newspaper printed what he said," she interjected. "And they said Brandon was very close to God and that's what keeps him going."

I thought back to what kept me going at Brandon's age, knowing that it certainly wasn't God. I didn't trust Jesus as my Savior until much later. Life was all about me and trying to be cool. Brandon had a peace about him and an unmistakable glint in his eye — like he knew the secret to what life was truly about.

As I watched Brandon speak, some verses from Psalms came to mind, "For the Lord God is a sun and shield. The Lord gives grace and glory; He does not withhold the good from those who live with integrity" (Psalm 84:11, HCSB).

Here was a young man who, medically speaking, could've died numerous times over, yet through God's grace was living to the fullest. The Lord had acted as a shield for Brandon, protecting him and giving him the grace to survive one more day.

Brandon has not only received grace from God, but he also lets it overflow into the lives of people around him. The Bible calls us "Christ's ambassadors"[24] after we accept the gift of God's grace. And Brandon takes that calling seriously as he spreads the good news of Jesus any way he can.

"What goes through your mind when you have the opportunity to share about God's grace?" I asked.

"Awesome! Thanks, God!" Brandon nearly shouted. "I just like to talk to people. And I always look for an opportunity to tell them about God."

Those opportunities come when he visits nursing homes and develops relationships with the elderly residents. Brandon's always gotten along with people who are older than he. In middle school, many of his friends were already in high school. They'd come over to watch movies or play video games.

"Have you met other Christian kids in the hospital?" I said.

"Most of them have already gone to be with Jesus," Brandon said matter-of-factly. "One that has stayed is Landon. He had a kidney transplant. But then he got an immune deficiency. When we got hooked up to the IVs for treatments, which can last from three to six hours, we tried to get chairs right next to each other. Then we could play with each other and have fun, forgetting about the IVs and all the noise."

"What is school like for you?"

"Because I'm homeschooled, I get to do a lot with science and math. I love to do science experiments to learn about how God designed the world. This may be a little gross, but I had three hermit crabs at home until one died. I wanted to figure out what made him die, so I put him in a Petri dish that I thought was airtight. When my mom came into my room to hook me up to my regular night feeds, she said, 'Brandon, what's that smell?' I didn't know. Then she said, 'Brandon, it's your crab!'"

"Did you study it under a microscope?"

"No. My mom said I had to throw it away."

"*Ha!* She's a smart lady," I said. "Speaking of smart, you read a lot, especially your Bible. Do you have a favorite Bible story?"

"Job is one of my favorites because he never blamed God no matter what God allowed Satan to do to him. He had boils. He lost his whole family. His friends betrayed him. He lived in a dump — but he never blamed God for any of it. He always trusted him."

"How about a favorite verse?"

"John 3:16," Brandon quickly answered. "'For God so loved the world that he gave his one and only Son, that whoever believes in him shall not perish but have eternal life.' I used to write that verse in big letters on poster board and tape it on the door of my hospital rooms. I wanted everybody to see it.

"God can use you in any circumstance no matter what your age or your health or whatever your life is like. He'll give you opportunities to evangelize to different people, and you should use those."

MOUNTAINTOP EXPERIENCE

My friend Jesse told me he couldn't stop thinking about this young evangelist. Brandon's body may be battling against itself, but there's no war between his heart and mind. Both are solely focused on telling others about Jesus.

The apostle Paul was the same way. In Acts 20:24, Paul writes, "my life means nothing to me. I only want to finish the race. I want to complete the work the Lord Jesus has given me. He wants me to give witness to others about the good news of God's grace" (NIrV).

Read the last line of that verse again, but personalize it for yourself: "The Lord Jesus wants (fill in your name) to give witness to others about the good news of God's grace."

As I (Lee) thought about the daily challenges Brandon faced, another aspect of the apostle Paul's life came to mind. Shortly after Jesus died on the cross, Paul met the risen Lord on the road to Damascus — an event that totally changed the course of Paul's life. It even changed his name, from Saul to Paul. From that point on, Paul traveled the world to tell others about Jesus. He went on three missionary journeys, all recorded in the book of Acts. In fact, most of the books in the New Testament are letters Paul wrote to the early Christian churches. Paul faced plenty of physical challenges. He was thrown in jail, beaten, shipwrecked, and had rocks thrown at him.

In Paul's second letter to the church in Corinth, he talks about a "thorn in the flesh" — mostly likely a physical ailment — that he lived with on a daily basis because the Lord wouldn't take it away. Paul pleaded with God three times to take away this physical challenge.[25] But God answered, "My grace is sufficient for you, for my power is made perfect in weakness." So instead of complaining about his weakness, Paul embraced it. He understood that's how God made him.

That's exactly the way that Brandon sees his life too. As I write this chapter, Brandon's no longer the twelve-year-old that Jesse met years ago. Now in his early twenties, Brandon still struggles with his medical conditions. His intestines are so messed up that he can't rely on getting his nutrition from eating or feeding tubes, so he has to get fed intravenously. Two recent blood infections nearly took his life. And chronic swelling in his brain has occasionally caused dementia-like symptoms, making it impossible for him to hold a conversation. These more scary episodes have been controlled by high-dose IV medications, which allow Brandon to continue communicating clearly — especially when it comes to his love and reliance on Jesus.

By relying on God's sufficient grace, Brandon's ability to witness for Christ remains strong. He runs his church's library, preaches sermons at the nursing home, and has taken on the church's card ministry where he writes more than 900 birthday cards to prisoners — not to mention Christmas and Easter cards — to let them know that God loves them and they're still cared for.

"It's not about my strength," Brandon wrote in a recent email. "But all through Christ."

To me, that sounded a lot like the apostle Paul's words in Philippians 4:13, "I can do everything by the power of Christ. He gives me strength" (NIrV).

Through God's grace, he gives us his power. Power to tell people about him. Power to face the toughest struggles.

Like the apostle Paul and Brandon, we'll all face hard times, be insulted, and experience difficulties. When those struggles come, don't fight through under your own strength. Instead tap into the power of God's grace, because "when I am weak, then I am strong" (2 Corinthians 12:10). Brandon lives out that verse. Hearing his story was definitely a mountaintop experience, but I knew I still had a long way to climb before I could fully comprehend the fullness of God's grace.

Face-to-Face with Grace

1. Do you think children handle being sick better than adults? Why?

2. When is the last time you told somebody about Jesus? How can understanding God's grace make you more bold to tell others about him?

Chapter 6 THE EXECUTIONER

ARE WE EVER BEYOND THE REACH OF GRACE?

I had come a long way in piecing together the riddle of grace. Stephanie Fast reminded me how God's grace doesn't just forgive, but it clears the way for us to be adopted into his family for all time. Andrew Palau showed me that our heavenly Father is patient, waiting for us to confess our wrongdoings and run back into his open arms of grace. Craig Hazen affirmed that in a world of different religions, Christianity stands alone as a beacon of grace. Brandon Rys demonstrated that grace provides us the strength to make it through life's challenges, giving us the boldness to tell others about an amazing God.

But are there limits on grace? Surely, God must draw the line somewhere. If there were ever a case of grace going too far, where God shakes his head and turns his back, I knew it would be found in the story told by Christopher LaPel.

Christopher's story sounds like a Hollywood film. The tale begins with a Cambodian child's innocent wish for a unfamiliar symbol. Then it winds through a confusing maze of horrors before ending in a prison with no hope of escape, occupied by an inmate with no hope except Christ.

Small and wearing rimless glasses, his hair black with no gray, Christopher sat casually in a wooden chair in his Los Angeles office as he calmly told me a fascinating tale of evil and survival.

"I grew up in Phnom Penh, Cambodia, where my father was a Buddhist high priest and spiritual advisor to Prince Norodom Sihanouk," he said, his voice heavily accented.

"My dad wanted me to take his position someday. When I was young, sometimes he would take me to the palace, where I would play with the prince's children. One day I saw some craftsmen. I said, 'Would you make me a cross out of ivory?' "

"A cross?" I asked. "Why would a Buddhist child ask for a cross?"

"I don't really know why. Maybe it was because I saw one on a church. My siblings had idols, but for some reason I was fixated on getting a cross. To me, it represented power and purity. The craftsman made the cross. I put it on a gold chain. It hung right here, under my shirt," he said, tapping his heart.

"How did your father react?" I said.

"Nobody could see it, until one day we were eating a meal as a family," Christopher said. "We sat on the floor with food in the center. When I reached to get something, the cross fell out of my shirt. Everyone looked. My dad was angry. He cursed at me in front of my brothers and sisters. He pulled me toward him and said, 'You shouldn't wear that cross! Remember, we are a Buddhist family.' "

"Did he punish you?" I said.

"Afterward, he apologized, but he said he didn't like the cross. He offered to make me any idol I wanted. I said, 'No, I don't want anything else.' Then he said, 'Next time, take it off.' After that, I moved the cross from my front to my back."

Christopher was wearing the cross on April 17, 1975, when Pol Pot's communist forces, called the Khmer Rouge, took over and forcibly emptied Cambodia's towns and cities. They burst into Christopher's home with assault rifles and said, "You have to leave. Don't take anything. In three days, you will come back."

Christopher and his family joined a flood of residents who clogged the narrow roads — walking, running, some riding bicycles or scooters, carrying everything they could. There was mass confusion and panic.

"Everyone was scared. I was nineteen years old at the time," Christopher said. "I was terrified. My dad said, 'Just do what they ask.' Three days turned into three weeks. Then we realized ... we would never get back home."

So began their quest to avoid the Killing Fields.

MYSTERY OF THE CROSS

Over the next 1,364 days, the Khmer Rouge killed, starved, or worked to death about two million

Cambodians. Nearly one out of four people in Cambodia died.

"Teachers – dead. Former government workers – dead. Journalists – dead," Christopher said to me. "They wanted to get rid of anyone who was educated. A friend of mine admitted to the Khmer Rouge that he was in college. He disappeared."

Out of 11,000 university students at the time, only 450 survived. As for doctors, nine out of ten were killed.[26] Money was abolished, personal property was taken away, schools closed, courts shut down, and religious practices were crushed.[27]

In other words, it was an entire nation without grace.

"The Khmer Rouge would question us," Christopher said. "We had to be careful. One slip and we were dead. They would say, 'Who are you? Have you been to school?' They shoved a notebook in front of us. 'Here. Write your name.'"

Christopher wrote his name with his left hand, so it would look awkward. Separated from his family, Christopher worked in the fields to grow rice and build canals as part of a grand strategy to construct a massive irrigation system and increase rice production. He worked twelve to fourteen hours a day. At night during the summer, he toiled by moonlight. Food was a watery soup, supplemented by lizards he would catch. His weight dropped to ninety pounds. His hair fell out from malnutrition. At night, the Khmer Rouge would call out names and people would disappear from their huts, never to be seen again.

"Sometime in late 1977, I got very sick with a high fever," Christopher said. "I missed three days of work. One night, a voice called my name. It was the Khmer Rouge. They dragged me from my hut. That was it. I knew I would be killed. I was scared. I was trembling.

"They told me to sit on the floor and asked why I hadn't been working. I told them I was sick but had no food or medicine. One said, 'What kind of sick are you?' I said, 'I have a high fever.' Someone said, 'Let's see how sick you are.'

"They began checking me. One put his hand on my head. Another placed a hand on my shoulder. Then one opened my shirt to put his hand on my chest, and that exposed the cross, hanging by a string. The light reflected off the ivory. There was silence; it seemed for a long time. Then there was a voice from somebody I couldn't see. He said, 'Well, this guy is really sick. We'll let him go.'"

I was inching toward the edge of my seat as

Christopher told the story. "Thank God!" I said. "But why did they react that way to the cross?"

"I don't know. They told me to go rest. The next day they gave me Chinese medicine and rice soup and treated me very well. A few days later, I got better. I don't know what it was about that cross, but I believe it saved my life."

Still, the struggle to stay alive in the rice fields became increasingly difficult. The workload increased as the food supply diminished. The brutality of the Khmer Rouge was relentless.

Christopher thought about it and decided he had nothing to lose by running away. In early 1979, he made a dash for the safety of Thailand. He escaped at night, navigating the jungle by moonlight. Eventually, he arrived at a refugee camp that was called by a name he didn't quite understand: Christian Outreach.

"I was so relieved, so happy to be there," he said. "I felt safe for the first time in so long. Then one day a woman shared with me about Jesus Christ. She talked about how he had died on the cross. I thought, *The cross?* I said, 'Tell me the meaning of the cross. Why did he die?' She told me how he died so I could be saved from my sins.

"At that moment, I remembered my ivory

cross and how God saved my life when I was sick. I prayed, 'Lord, I was supposed to die that night, but you spared me. I want to commit my life to serving you, no matter what you want me to do. My life is yours.'"

Christopher reached his hand up to feel the cross around his neck, but it was gone. Somewhere in the jungle, the string had broken. He grinned at the memory. "I had lost the cross," he said, "but I had found Jesus."

In the camp Christopher met and fell in love with another refugee named Vanna. They were married. In 1980, they immigrated to the United States, where Vanna had a sister. Christopher graduated from a school fittingly named Hope International University and became pastor of Golden West Christian Church in Los Angeles. That's where I was sitting with him in his second-floor office.

Christopher has never forgotten Cambodia. He continues to go back to his homeland to train and equip Christians. Today, more than 200 churches have been started in Cambodia because of his ministry.

THE HORROR OF S-21

Many members of Christopher's family were not as lucky. When he talks about them, his voice becomes softer. At times, I had to strain to hear him.

While he was still held captive in Cambodia, he learned the Khmer Rouge had worked his father and mother to death. His sister, who was a broadcaster in the capital city, was slain. His brother was killed shortly before Vietnamese-led rebel forces came in 1979 to push out Pol Pot.

"Then there was my cousin," he said.

"Tell me about her," I said.

He hesitated. "She was a scientist who taught at a school." Pause. "She was arrested and taken to S-21."

The infamous S-21 was a four-building compound that the Khmer Rouge used as an questioning, torture, and execution center. The "S" stood for *sala*, which means hall, and the "21" is the code for *santebal*, or security police.[28]

People who lived nearby only knew the facility as *konlaenh choul min dael chenh* — "the place where people go in but never come out."[29] A Khmer Rouge slogan summed up their strategy: "Better to destroy ten innocent people than to let one enemy go free."[30]

Kaing Guek Eav, better known as Comrade Duch (pronounced *Doik*), was a former mathematics teacher who directed the institution with chilling cruelty.[31] He put together records of every torture session, every forced confession, and every murder.

All prisoners were photographed when they arrived. On a list of eight teenagers and nine children, Duch wrote the order: "Kill them all."[32] More than 14,000 prisoners entered S–21; only seven people are known to have survived.

When the Khmer Rouge was defeated by a band of Cambodians backed by the Vietnamese in 1979, Duch didn't have time to destroy the records before he fled. He disappeared and was thought dead.

Christopher's cousin and her boyfriend were buried in shallow graves near the terrible compound.

"I weep when I think of what happened to her," Christopher said. "S–21 is now a genocide museum. Her youngest brother took me there in 1993. There are hundreds of mug shots of prisoners on the walls. We found the picture of my cousin."

He blinked away tears. His body language was clear. He didn't want to say anything more about it.

A LIFE TRANSFORMED

In 1994, fifteen years after Cambodia was freed from the unthinkable evil of Pol Pot's communist rule, Christopher and a team from his congregation bought farmland and built a church in the northwestern part of the country. The following year he returned to Cambodia for two weeks to run leadership training among a hundred local Christians.

One of his key leaders invited a friend, Hang Pin, who was a teacher in a village not far away. Hang was in his mid fifties and scrawny. His most unique physical trait was that his ears stuck out. He spoke Thai, some English, and had taught the Khmer language for a while at the Foreign Languages Institute in Beijing, China.

Although he wasn't a Christian, Hang agreed to attend Christopher's training because he was suffering from depression and looking for encouragement.

"He was shy, quiet, very withdrawn and discouraged, and sitting in the back," Christopher recalled.

Typically, Christopher would end his sessions with an altar call, asking those who wanted to receive the forgiveness of Christ to come forward.

Most there already followed Jesus, so generally not many people responded. At the end of one class, Christopher was surprised to see that Hang had joined several others in stepping forward.

"I said to him, 'I'd like to pray for you. Do you have anything to say?'"

"What did he tell you?" I asked.

"He said he had done a lot of bad things in his life and didn't know if his brothers and sisters could forgive the sins he'd committed. He was sorry. He was remorseful."

"Did you ask for any details?" I said.

"No, I was more concerned about the present: Was he repentant, and did he understand forgiveness is a gift of God's grace? And yes, he did. I told him, 'God loves you. He can forgive you.' I prayed with him, and the next day I baptized him in the Sangke River. Rarely have I seen such an immediate transformation in anyone."

"Really? How so?" I asked.

"His attitude, his demeanor—everything changed," Christopher said. "Now he was sitting in the front row. He was dressed more neatly. He was excited. He would ask questions and interact with enthusiasm. He couldn't get enough teaching. He was the most attentive of all the students. He took detailed notes and read the Bible eagerly. He couldn't wait to start a church in his village."

Before long, Hang received his certificate for completing the training. "I remember when we took our group picture," Christopher said. "He was standing right next to me in the front row. I put my hand on his shoulder."

Later, Christopher heard that Hang had returned to his village, led his children to Christ, and baptized them. "After that he planted a house church," Christopher said. "Soon there were fourteen families. We continued to be in contact, and he came back for more leadership training."

Two years later, uprooted by violence in his area, Hang ended up in Ban Ma Muang, a camp with 12,000 refugees inside Thailand. He began to serve with the American Refugee Committee (ARC), training health workers and saving countless lives by helping stem a typhoid outbreak.[33] An ARC official called him "our best worker, highly respected in the community, clearly very intelligent, and dedicated to helping the refugees."[34]

When violence stopped in Cambodia, Hang returned and worked closely with World Vision, the Christian aid ministry, to provide health care to women and children. Over time, Christopher and Hang lost track of each other. That is, until a phone call woke up Christopher in his Los Angeles home in April 1999.

THE CALL THAT CHANGED EVERYTHING

The caller identified himself as a reporter for the Associated Press. "Could you help us identify one of your teachers?" he asked.

"Many people have come through my training," Christopher replied.

The reporter described this individual – not very tall, skinny, his ears sticking out.

"Yes, I know him," Christopher said. "Hang Pin. He's one of our lay pastors."

"Well, he was one of the top Khmer Rouge," the reporter said.

Christopher's mouth dropped open. "What do you mean?"

"He's a mass murderer. He was in charge of S–21. Hang Pin is Comrade Duch!"

Christopher fell to his knees and slapped his forehead. His mind raced from his murdered cousin to the S–21 museum to baptizing Hang Pin. *Is this possible? How can this be?*

Slowly, the story emerged. Photojournalist Nic Dunlop had tracked down Duch in his jungle village. Then he and investigative reporter Nate

Thayer, who had previously questioned Pol Pot, confronted Duch about who he was.[35]

At first, Duch tried to hide the truth. But quickly he began admitting his past. "It is God's will you are here," Duch said to them. "Now my future is in God's hands. I have done very bad things in my life. Now it is time for *les represailles* [for me to bear the consequences] of my actions."

Dunlop and Thayer showed Duch copies of the documents he had signed to authorize executions.

"I am so sorry. The people who died were good people," Duch said, tears in his eyes. "My fault is that I didn't serve God. I served men. I served communism. I feel very sorry about the killings and the past."

Now, he said, he had a new goal: "I want to tell everyone about the good news of Jesus Christ."

Duch readily confessed to his crimes and said he would testify against other Khmer Rouge officials so that they, too, could be brought to justice. Knowing he would be arrested and jailed, Duch said: "It is okay. They have my body. Jesus has my soul. It is important that this history be understood. I want to tell you everything clearly."

Duch gave himself to the authorities and eventually was put on trial before a United

Nations panel of judges for crimes against humanity (people and humans in general), murder, and torture. He didn't hide from his past as other Khmer Rouge killers were trying to do.

His testimony made headlines around the world because of his clear-cut confession of his offenses. "I am responsible for the crimes committed at S–21, especially the torture and execution of the people there," he told the five-judge panel. "May I be permitted to apologize to the survivors of the regime and families of the victims who had loved ones who died brutally at S–21."[36]

At one point, Duch agreed to be taken in handcuffs back to the blood-splattered S–21 to face his accusers. He collapsed in tears, saying, "I ask for your forgiveness. I know that you cannot forgive me, but I ask you to leave me the hope that you might."

One of the few S–21 survivors exclaimed: "Here are the words that I have longed to hear for thirty years!"[37]

Convicted of his crimes, Duch today is locked in a prison in Phnom Penh for the rest of his life. The ruling is final. The judicial system allows no appeal.

Christopher and the lay pastor he knew as Hang Pin came face-to-face in 2008, after Duch had already spent nine years in military detention awaiting trial. A lawyer for the international courts had arranged the meeting at Duch's prison in Phnom Penh.

"What was the very first thing you said to him?" I asked Christopher.

"I said, 'Before we start, I want to tell you that I love you as my brother in Christ. I forgive you for what you've done to my family.'"

"It was as easy as that?" I asked, snapping my fingers.

He shook his head. "No, not easy – necessary. I had a long time to think and pray about this beforehand. How could I receive forgiveness from Christ for my sins but at the same time refuse to forgive someone for their sins, no matter how terrible?"

"How did he respond?"

"In his eyes, I saw tears," Christopher said. "As for me, I felt joy and peace in that moment. I felt liberated."

"What happened then?" I asked.

"We prayed together. After that, we praised God and I served him communion. I read the Bible out loud from Psalm 23."

The familiar passage came to my mind: "*The Lord is my shepherd, I lack nothing.... You prepare a table before me in the presence of my enemies....*"

I asked, "Did you talk about what happened at S–21?"

"No, I'm his pastor, not his prosecutor. Duch told me, 'The Holy Spirit has convicted my heart. I have to tell the world what I've done to my people. I will tell the truth, and the truth will set me free.'"

Since then, whenever Christopher makes one of his journeys to Cambodia, he goes to the prison to meet with Duch. Because of his status as a pastor, Christopher is one of the few visitors allowed to see the inmate. He has brought Cambodian Bibles, a book of worship songs, and a communion set to Duch. Each Sunday, as part of his own private worship session in a prison without any other Christians, Duch serves himself communion.

"Since his conviction and sentence to life in prison, what is his demeanor?" I asked.

"When he sees me, he runs up to me, tears in his eyes. He is joyful. He is peaceful. Yes, he carries the weight of his crimes, but he is so thankful for God's grace. He is sharing Jesus with the guards and the other prisoners who are former Khmer

Rouge. He tells them there's forgiveness available for them as well."

"What does he say to you?"

"He told me, 'I'm not a prisoner; I'm a free man. I rejoice every day of my life. I deserve death. I deserve this punishment. But I have Jesus, and so I have love. If I had Jesus before, I never would have done what I did. I never knew about his love.'"

BREAKING THE CYCLE

"To a lot of people, it doesn't seem fair that Duch could be forgiven for the brutality of his crimes," I said. "They'd want him to be miserable on earth and die alone."

"Grace is not fair," Christopher said. "And everyone should be grateful for that, not just Duch. Jesus' death has infinite value because he's an infinite God. It covers all the sins of the world. If we say some sin is too terrible, then we're saying Jesus fell short in his mission. Grace is only grace if it's available even to the Duchs of the world. In fact," he said, straightening himself in his chair, "here's a difficult thing for us to comprehend: God loves Duch as much as he loves you and me."

I allowed myself to feel the full impact of that statement. "That *is* hard to accept," I said.

Christopher continued. "The truth is that God looked beneath the filth that covered Duch's life and saw a core that is made in his image. That image is obscured but never destroyed. When the Bible says God loves the world, it doesn't footnote any exceptions. God's grace is inexhaustible.

"Perhaps we don't think we need as much grace as Duch does, because our sins aren't as horrible. We conveniently forget our daily rebellions against God's teachings. No, we don't deserve grace, and neither does Duch. For each of us, it is a gift."

I asked him what the rest of Cambodia thinks. "Do they believe that even Duch could be redeemed?"

"Many are hearing of his strong faith and saying, 'Look how God can change a life,'" Christopher said. "They are surprised he would admit his guilt and humbly ask forgiveness. They're saying, 'Look at these Christians. They are forgiving. Why can't we do that too?' I think, in the end, this will help the churches in Cambodia. God is opening up hearts and minds to see that Jesus is love and that he can bring healing and hope.

"That's very important," he continued, "because grace is unknown in Buddhism. So many Cambodians hold in their hatred and anger. They don't know how to release it. Someday, it might erupt into another era of violence. Maybe if Cambodians can learn about forgiveness through the story of Duch, it can break the cycle. What else but grace can do that?"

Face-to-Face with Grace

1. Do you think there's anything you could do that would change God's love for you? What does this teach you about God's grace?

2. Is it harder for you to forgive yourself or other people's actions toward you? Why?

Chapter 7
THE HERO

WHAT DOES GRACE LOOK LIKE IN ACTION?

Around 26 million students ride the bus to school every day across the United States.[38] Normally, these trips aren't very newsworthy. No TV station would ever report a story proclaiming: "Everybody Arrived Safely at School."

But on the morning of April 9, 2012, one bus ride grabbed national attention.

The day started like any other typical Monday for Jeremy.[39] Spring break had just finished for the seventh grader. He and his classmates sat on the school bus talking about what they'd done during their time away from the classroom.

Suddenly, from his seat in the second row, Jeremy heard the bus driver start to choke. Jeremy turned and saw the driver's body twitch and then slump over, causing the bus to veer dangerously off the road.

Screams filled the bus. Other students crouched in fear. Nobody seemed to know what to do — except Jeremy. He jumped from his seat and ran to the front of the bus.

Bus surveillance cameras show the thirteen-year-old grabbing the wheel, jerking the bus to the right to get it back on the road, and pulling the keys out of the ignition to turn off the engine. While Jeremy steered the bus until it came to a stop, one of his Surprise Lake Middle School classmates ran forward to start chest compressions on the driver. Johnny had gone through CPR training the previous summer and could tell the bus driver needed medical attention fast.

The bus came to rest a few blocks from school,

and almost immediately an adult ran onto the bus to continue lifesaving measures on the driver.

The heroics of these two boys quickly spread across the nation. Their local newspaper interviewed Jeremy and Johnny, and they even appeared on the *Today Show* several days later.

With close-cropped brown hair and light brown eyes, Jeremy deflected attention from himself. Instead of basking in the glory that people heaped on him because of his courageous actions, he didn't want to take too much credit. Then he said something that really stood out.

"The bus was going on the curb, and there's a church at the end of the curb," Jeremy explained to the interviewer. "I'm a Christian. And I didn't want to hit a church."[40]

In front of a national audience of millions and sitting next to his mom on a couch, Jeremy boldly proclaimed he was a Christ follower. During his fifteen minutes of fame, Jeremy pointed to Jesus.

Once I learned about Jeremy, I knew I had to hear more of his story. Jeremy's actions demonstrated a different part of God's grace. This was grace under fire.

Other students panicked or didn't know what to do, but God gave Jeremy the grace to remain calm, make wise decisions, and ultimately, save the day. I saw a story about Jeremy in the October 2012 issue of *Focus on the Family Clubhouse* magazine. The magazine had interviewed Jeremy about a month after the incident at his home in the Pacific Northwest to get the whole story.[41] I asked for the full scoop, and here's what I got.

TAKING THE WHEEL

Connecting with Jeremy after his rise into the national spotlight wasn't easy. But once the family discovered a Christian magazine wanted the interview, they called right back. Jeremy had mentioned his faith in Jesus Christ in many interviews he'd done, but the writers had always edited that part out before printing the story. Only when he said it live on the *Today Show* did people hear how Jeremy's faith influenced his actions. That's exactly the story *Clubhouse* wanted to tell.

Clubhouse: What goes through a person's mind when he jumps into action during a dangerous situation? Most of the kids on the bus looked pretty scared, yet you ran up the aisle. What made you do it?

Jeremy: It all happened really fast. I'm just sitting around on a normal day, and then suddenly I'm at the wheel trying to steer the bus away from a church. I didn't have a lot of time to think about what to do. I just sprang into action. I steered the bus to the side of the road and took the keys out of the ignition. I tried doing CPR on the driver, but I didn't know how. Then Johnny came up and said he knew CPR. So he did CPR, and I ran to get someone's phone to call 9-1-1. But someone already called.

Clubhouse: How long did it take paramedics and the police to get there?

Jeremy: I'm not sure. One of my former principals, Mr. McCrossin, was driving behind the bus. He saw everything that happened. Almost right away after we stopped, he got on the bus and told us all to walk to school, because we were right next to it. So I actually didn't see.

Clubhouse: On the *Today Show*, you said you were a Christian. What does that mean to you?

Jeremy: That means I get to know the actual God — *the one true God* in the whole world. And I get to know all the great works he's done and what awaits me when I die.

Clubhouse: Were you praying as you ran up and drove the bus?

Jeremy: Afterward, I prayed for the bus driver to recover, but he didn't. I feel kind of bad.

Nothing like that's happened to anybody I've known.

Because of Jeremy's and Johnny's quick response, plus the efforts of John McCrossin and the paramedics, the bus driver was revived and taken to the hospital. However, the driver later died. Jeremy explained that he turned to God for peace, and members of his church came around his family to pray and encourage him.

Hearing his story made me appreciate the grace God gives us to deal with tragedies in our lives. We may not always understand why something happens, but through God's grace we can find peace when we turn to him. Being part of God's family can also give us strength. Jeremy's mom noted that the church youth group was a real support.

Clubhouse: How did God protect and help you during this time?

Jeremy: Well, first, God protected me from hitting a church. I know that for sure. Because if I didn't go to the wheel, then that church would have had a big hole in it and the bus would have been ruined and a lot more injuries could have occurred.

Clubhouse: How has it been, getting all of this attention?

Jeremy: From my point of view, I've done a whole bunch of interviews — like five or ten. They made some announcements over the PA at school. Then the mayor of Milton and the chief of police gave me a gold coin for what I did. All of the kids on Bus 29 were called up in front of the school. But Johnny and I received a coin. And probably everybody knows I'm a Christian now.

TAKING ACTION

After learning more about Jeremy, a verse from the apostle Peter popped into my head. Peter, just like Jeremy, was a man of action. Peter courageously leapt from a boat to walk on water toward Jesus. And it worked ... until he took his eyes off the Savior and started to sink.[42] Later in his life, Peter chopped off a servant's ear with his sword when Jesus was arrested in the garden of Gethsemane.[43] Peter is also the disciple who denied he knew Jesus three times in one night!

When our words and actions, through the power of God's grace, reflect Jesus, people notice. That's what happened to Peter. As he hung out in the dark near Jesus' trial, people recognized him and said, "Aren't you one of his disciples?" Three times, Peter replied, "I am not."[44]

GRACE-FILLED LAUGHS

Q What do you get when you combine a praying mantis and a termite?

A An insect that says grace before it eats your house.

Q What is a horse's favorite hymn?

A "A-*neigh*-zing Grace."

A man was walking through the African savannah when two lions jumped from the tall grass and started chasing him. He ran as fast as he could, but ended up at the edge of a cliff. In desperation, he dropped to his knees and prayed, "Dear God, please let these lions be Christian lions."

To the man's amazement, one of the lions stood on its hind legs, walked over, and put its paw on the man's head. But the man's relief quickly changed when the lion said, "Thank you, Lord, for this meal we're about to receive."

Jeremy did the opposite by standing up for his Savior and saying, "I am a Christian." In Jesus' famous Sermon on the Mount, he told the crowds not to hide their light under a bushel. Instead their light should be placed on a stand for everybody to see.[45]

Soon after denying Christ, Peter met the risen Lord and started shining his light for Jesus. He went on to become a powerful preacher. Once Peter talked to a large crowd, and 3,000 people accepted Christ as their Savior at one time![46]

Peter understood God's grace—the grace that comes with being forgiven for wrong actions and gives courage to act boldly. In 1 Peter 1:13, he wrote, "With minds that are alert and fully sober, set your hope on the grace to be brought to you when Jesus Christ is revealed at his coming."

The more deeply I dug into grace, the more I realized what a difference it makes in the world. Grace comforts. Grace strengthens. Grace gives hope. Through God's grace, we don't need to be afraid—no matter what situation we find ourselves in, even if that's saying we're a Christian or sitting on an out-of-control school bus.

Face-to-Face with Grace

1. Have you ever been in a situation where you had to act boldly, trusting in God's grace? If so, what did you do?

2. Read Acts 6:8. What connection do you see between God's grace and power? Does one lead to the other? How?

Chapter 8
THE THIEF

EXPERIENCING GOD'S GRACE CHANGES OUR ETERNITY

Jesus didn't come to earth to be a hero. Yet his actions, through God's grace, made him one. Jesus didn't think of himself. He was solely focused on others. When life got dangerous, God's Son boldly walked forward, giving his life on the cross so we could be forgiven of our sins and live with him in heaven.

Jesus' sacrifice makes him the ultimate hero. He has rescued more people from the flames than any fireman. He has turned more lives around for God than any preacher. When we meet him and understand what he did for us, it can change our lives forever — just like it did for a little girl I met years ago.[47]

LIFE LESSON FROM A LITTLE GIRL

When I worked full-time as a pastor, a friend called with what he said was an embarrassing confession: His little girl had been caught shoplifting from our church bookstore. He wanted to know if I would represent the church so she could come and apologize. I'd never had to do anything like this before, but I agreed.

The next day, the parents and their eight-year-old daughter trooped into my office and sat down. "Tell me what happened," I said to the little girl as gently as I could.

"Well," she said as she started to sniffle, "I was in the bookstore after a service. I saw a book that I really wanted, but I didn't have any money ..." Tears formed in her eyes and spilled down her cheeks. I handed her a tissue. "So I put the book under my coat and took it. I knew it was wrong. I knew I shouldn't do it, but I did. And I'm sorry. I'll never do it again. Honest!"

"I'm so glad you're willing to admit what you did and say you're sorry," I told her. "That's very brave, and it's the right thing to do. But what do you think an appropriate punishment would be?"

She shrugged her shoulders.

I thought for a moment, then said, "I understand the book cost five dollars. I think it would be fair if you paid the bookstore five dollars, plus three times that amount, which would make the total twenty dollars. Do you think that would be fair?"

She nodded sadly. "Yes," she murmured. But now there was fear in her eyes. Twenty dollars was a mountain of money to an eight-year-old. Where would she ever come up with that much cash?

As I watched her mind spin and more tears fall down her cheeks, I pulled open my desk drawer, removed my checkbook, and wrote out a check from my personal account for the full amount. I tore off the check and handed it to her. Her mouth dropped open.

"I'm going to pay your penalty so you don't have to. Do you know why I'd do that?" Bewildered, she shook her head. "Because I love you. Because I care about you. Because you're valuable to me. And please remember this: That's how Jesus feels about you too. Except to an even higher degree."

I wish I could find the words to describe the look of absolute relief and joy that blossomed on her face! She was almost giddy with gratitude.

That's a bit like the offer Jesus makes to you. By his suffering and death on the cross, he paid the complete penalty for your wrongdoings, as your substitute, so you wouldn't have to. Out of his love for you, he's offering that payment for all your sins as a pure gift – which you're free to accept or reject.

You can't earn God's grace. Your actions have nothing to do with it. It's not about who you are. It's all about who God is. No story better illustrates this than one about a different thief. Instead of a young shoplifter, this thief died next to Jesus on a cross.

When the Romans crucified Christ, the Bible says two criminals were also killed. One hung on Jesus' left. The other was on his right.

One of the criminals joined in with the people mocking Jesus. He shouted, "Aren't you the Messiah? Save yourself and us!"[48]

But the other criminal looked over at Jesus

and knew the truth. He yelled back at the first criminal, "Don't you fear God ...? We are punished justly, for we are getting what our deeds deserve. But this man has done nothing wrong."

Then he turned to Jesus and quietly said, "Jesus, remember me when you come into your kingdom."

Jesus looked back at the man. This thief knew he deserved to die. We don't know what crimes he committed or what people he may have hurt. Jesus didn't care about the man's past. But Jesus certainly knew about this man's future – he was going to die on a cross. This thief couldn't do any great things for God on earth. He had nothing to give ... except an apologetic heart that asked for forgiveness, knowing it was only something God could give.

The Bible doesn't say how much time passed between the thief's words and Jesus' answer. It just says, "Jesus answered him, 'Truly I tell you, today you will be with me in paradise.'"

Just like the people who witnessed Jesus dying on the cross, it's your choice whether you believe that Jesus is the Son of God. Some mocked. Others asked for forgiveness. If you've never prayed to accept God's forgiveness, you can do that right now. Tell him that you believe in him. You can pray these words (or put them in your own thoughts):

Jesus, I'm sorry for all the times I've sinned. I know I deserve to be punished, and I believe you suffered and paid my debt by dying on the cross and rising from the dead. I accept your gift of forgiveness. Help me to follow you. Thank you for saving me and letting me live under your grace. Amen.

If you pray this prayer, tell someone: a parent, a youth pastor, or the person who gave you this book. There's no real risk in doing what that little girl did and taking a gift to pay a debt that you could never pay on your own. She admitted her wrongdoing because it was true and she was sorry. She took the check because she was powerless to pay the price herself.

Her reaction was the same one I often see on the faces of people who have received Christ's saving grace and ended up having a life-changing encounter with Jesus: there's joy, there's thankfulness, and most of all there's shock over God's outlandish grace.

Face-to-Face with Grace

1. Have you ever been caught doing something that you know you shouldn't? What was your punishment? Has anyone ever shown grace to you (your parents or a teacher or the person who caught you)? How?

2. Read Romans 5:1 – 2. Why is Christ's sacrifice so life changing when you have faith and believe in him?

LASSIE

Chapter 9

DREAM COME TRUE

WHEN ALL SEEMS LOST, GOD'S GRACE IS ENOUGH

I've never been a paranoid person. Working for a big-city newspaper, I'd met my share of shady characters. As a pastor at a megachurch, I'd made my share of enemies. But I'd never really worried about people eavesdropping on my conversations or plotting my downfall.

Then before a recent birthday, I started to have crazy thoughts: *That jogger going by the house — certainly he's working under cover for the FBI.*

Sounds funny, but back then it seemed to make total sense. This went on for days, with the fear and confusion getting increasingly worse. I had no idea I was suffering from *hyponatremia* — a medical condition where low salt levels in the blood become life threatening. Water was entering my body's cells and triggering dangerous swelling in my brain and unbelievably frightening thoughts.

One afternoon I sat down on the couch feeling sapped of all energy. I couldn't even lift an arm. The room began to darken. I felt like an ominous and evil presence filled the house. My heart raced. It was like I was descending into hell.

The room was cold and damp. I felt suffocated by hopelessness and despair. Menacing creatures began to gather at the corners of the room, slowly inching toward me. Snakes slithered on the floor. I wanted to lift my feet to escape, but I couldn't move. Deep inside, I felt what it was like to face eternity in this den of evil and terror. There was no hope of rescue. No way to escape. No relief from the panic.

I have no idea how long this experience lasted, but suddenly I heard the back door close. My wife walked into the kitchen and the disturbing images disappeared. I still sat on the couch, shaken and trying to figure out what just happened.

"You don't look well," my wife said as she sat down next to me. "Why don't you lie down for a while?"

Alone in the bedroom, my yet-to-be diagnosed hyponatremia continued to worsen. I became utterly convinced that everything in my life was gone. My wife was leaving me. My children hated me. My friends were abandoning me. My bank accounts were empty. The house and cars were being taken away. Police were hunting for me. I imagined myself living in a dirt field — alone and shivering against the Colorado cold, with nowhere to go and nobody to help me.

From my perspective, this was no fantasy. This was reality. I have since learned that these horrible visions are normal for someone suffering from hyponatremia. But I felt the full impact of being totally alone.

I wish I could say that my natural response was to seek Jesus, but it wasn't. As my brain was squeezed against the inside of my skull, my weird thoughts increased. In my complete confusion, I began to think that Jesus had abandoned me like everyone else.

RECONNECTING WITH GOD

The entire ordeal lasted several days. In the midst of it all, my son Kyle came to me with a simple suggestion: "Dad, we need to pray."

Kyle was a toddler when I came to faith in Jesus. He prayed to accept Christ as a young man and then felt called into ministry during a missions trip to the Dominican Republic, where he found himself in frightening situations during a time of civil unrest.

Kyle had carefully studied the Bible in college. He had dug into God's truth, especially the way we become more and more like Christ. It was his know-how in helping others in this way, and his concern for the confusion he could see growing in me, that urged his visit to our house.

Honestly, I didn't want to pray with him. I was feeling as if God had walked away from me, like everyone else in my imagination. Kyle and I sat next to each other.

"Dad, I don't know everything that's going on with you, but I sense you're feeling far from God right now," he said.

"That's true," I said.

"Well, I want to help you reconnect with who you are in Christ."

"What do you mean?"

"You see, when we approach God, we often bring a fake self," Kyle explained. "In this world our identity is tied up in what we do and what we accomplish. We hide who we really are and pretend to God — and to the world — that we're really in control. I want to help you get back to the truth."

I nodded. "I want that too."

For the next thirty minutes, Kyle guided me in a prayer. We prayed out loud. First, he'd say a line. Then I'd repeat it. I'd probably prayed words like this before, but Kyle's timing was perfect. This was exactly what I needed ... to see myself as God sees me.

Our time was filled with long pauses, as I thought about the truth of each statement. Kyle followed a prayer written by one of his professors that he had learned as he earned his doctoral degree.[49] I let the words soak into my soul before repeating them aloud to God.

"Lord, I admit I have sinned," Kyle began. "I am just a man. I like to believe I can control life and run my world, but the truth is I can't. Only you can.

"Right now I'm feeling confused and tired and scared. I can't make everyone happy. I can't even accomplish my own goals and desires. I'm thankful I'm not God. Only you can meet all of my needs."

Kyle paused before going on. Then, he talked about all of my accomplishments and possessions. Those are the things the world sees, but much of it is unimportant to God.

"I am not defined by my abilities, my roles, or my accomplishments," Kyle continued. "I am not defined by what other people think of me. At the core of my spirit, I'm not a pastor ... I'm not an author ... I'm not a speaker ... I'm not my awards or honors ... I'm not a Christian celebrity ... I'm not my possessions or my relationships."

As I prayed those words, I felt layers of myself peeling away. I was relieved. I could stop pretending. I could stop acting like I had all the answers. I could come into God's presence as I really was. (I'd encourage you to pray a prayer like this; just substitute the things that make up your world. For instance, "God, I'm not an honor student ... a soccer player ... a great musician ... I'm not a Bible memorization champion ... a talented writer ... the lead in the musical." You're not any of your roles or accomplishments in God's eyes. You're simply his child.)

"Lord," Kyle said, with me continuing to echo his words, "I affirm my true identity: I am yours, God, created for a relationship with you. I am precious in your eyes. I am fully forgiven of my sins and fully accepted by you. I am your son, beloved by you for eternity. Held in your everlasting embrace. *That* is who I truly am."

My eyes started to tear up as I realized the truth: Even if I were to actually lose everything — my house, my finances, my friends, my reputation, my position — it really wouldn't matter. Because in the end, I would still have God's grace. I would still be his adopted and beloved son. And that would be enough.

Our prayer continued for quite a while. At the end of our time together, Kyle picked up his Bible and read the apostle Paul's words in Philippians 3:8–9:

"I consider everything a loss because of the surpassing worth of knowing Christ Jesus my Lord, for whose sake I have lost all things. I consider them garbage, that I may gain Christ and be found in him, not having a righteousness of my own that comes from the law, but that which is through faith in Christ."

I thought of the angel in my childhood dream. Even though it had happened almost fifty years ago, I'd never forgotten what the angel had said in my dream. First, the angel had questioned my statement that I was going to heaven on my own merits. Then the angel said, "Someday you'll understand."

Back then, I didn't realize that my understanding would come in stages over time, as the depth and truth of God's grace unfolded in my life.

Now I had seen in my own life and in the lives of others that God accomplishes his purposes, even through the most painful of events. The dream of my twelve-year-old self had come true. I *understood.*

FREE, INDEED

Nothing is more freeing than grace. After my hyponatremia landed me in the hospital, doctors carefully raised the sodium levels in my blood back to normal. It had to be done slowly or my brain could have been permanently damaged. Doctors said I could have died.

Then one day my doctor came bounding into my room. "Everything's normal," he said. "You're free to go."

I smiled and glanced out the window at the

snowcapped Rocky Mountains. *I'm free, all right*, I thought to myself. *More than he knows.*

The doctors told me that this entire ordeal was a fluke, a weird combination of medical issues. The hallucinations? They're typical for severe hyponatremia cases. They wouldn't come back. And yet I knew they had left their mark.

After the hallucinations made me feel completely alone, penniless, and trapped, I would never see the homeless the same way again. Or the imprisoned. Or the abandoned. Or the weak.

And I would never see myself the same again. I was determined to cling to my true identity — a son of the Most High, amazed by God's grace.

Over and over, the Bible shouts: *God's love for me has no bounds and is unconditional. His grace is unending. I am his work and his pride. God can't stand the thought of spending all time without me in his family.*

As God's grace utterly rocked my life — forgiving me, adopting me, and changing my eternity — something else became clear: How tragic it would be to withhold the news of that grace from others. How could I enjoy and celebrate God's grace myself but never pass it along to a world that is dying to experience it?

What if Iris Eriksson had never picked

Stephanie off the trash heap? What if Luis Palau had never written letters to his son Andrew? What if Craig had never realized that even a good kid needs forgiveness? What if Brandon wallowed in self-pity, instead of boldly saying he was a Christian? What if the woman in the refugee camp had never revealed the meaning of the cross to Christopher? What if Jeremy had never said on national TV, "I am a Christian." As the apostle Paul asked, how can people believe in Christ if they have never heard about him?[50]

"[God] dispenses his goodness not with an eyedropper but a fire hydrant. Your heart is a Dixie cup and his grace is the Mediterranean Sea. You simply can't contain it all," popular pastor and writer Max Lucado said. "So let it bubble over. Spill out. Pour forth. 'Freely you have received, freely give.'"[51]

Writing about my journey of grace in this book has only strengthened my resolve to try to be like the apostle Paul. "What matters most to me," Paul wrote, "is to finish what God started: the job the Master Jesus gave me of letting everyone I meet know all about this incredibly extravagant generosity of God" (Acts 20:24 MSG).

That is the joyful task of every follower of Jesus, including me and including you. Someday may it be written of me: *He was so amazed by God's grace that he couldn't keep it to himself.*

May the same thing be written about you too.

Face-to-Face with Grace

1. Have you ever felt far away from God? Do you think you moved away from him or that he distanced himself from you? If you're not sure, read Deuteronomy 31:8 and Hebrews 13:8.

2. Where do you find your true identity – in your skills, accomplishments, and friends, or in Jesus Christ? Why?

WHAT THE BIBLE SAYS ABOUT GRACE

And I will pour out on the house of David and the inhabitants of Jerusalem a spirit of grace and supplication. They will look on me, the one they have pierced, and they will mourn for him as one mourns for an only child, and grieve bitterly for him as one grieves for a firstborn son. — *Zechariah 12:10*

And the child [Jesus] grew and became strong; he was filled with wisdom, and the grace of God was on him. — *Luke 2:40*

The Word became flesh and made his dwelling among us. We have seen his glory, the glory of the one and only Son, who came from the Father, full of grace and truth. — *John 1:14*

Out of his fullness we have all received grace in place of grace already given. — *John 1:16*

For the law was given through Moses; grace and truth came through Jesus Christ. — *John 1:17*

Now Stephen, a man full of God's grace and power, performed great wonders and signs among the people. — *Acts 6:8*

When he arrived and saw what the grace of God had done, he was glad and encouraged them all to remain true to the Lord with all their hearts. — *Acts 11:23*

When the congregation was dismissed, many of the Jews and devout converts to Judaism followed Paul and Barnabas, who talked with them and urged them to continue in the grace of God. — *Acts 13:43*

So Paul and Barnabas spent considerable time there, speaking boldly for the Lord, who confirmed the message of his grace by enabling them to perform signs and wonders. — *Acts 14:3*

We believe it is through the grace of our Lord Jesus that we are saved, just as they are. — *Acts 15:11*

When Apollos wanted to go to Achaia, the brothers and sisters encouraged him and wrote to the disciples there to welcome him. When he arrived, he was a great help to those who by grace had believed. — *Acts 18:27*

However, I consider my life worth nothing to me; my only aim is to finish the race and complete the task the Lord Jesus has given me — the task of testifying to the good news of God's grace. — *Acts 20:24*

Now I commit you to God and to the word of his grace, which can build you up and give you an inheritance among all those who are sanctified. — *Acts 20:32*

Through him we received grace and apostleship to call all the Gentiles to the obedience that comes from faith for his name's sake. — *Romans 1:5*

To all in Rome who are loved by God and called to be his holy people: Grace and peace to you from God our Father and from the Lord Jesus Christ. — *Romans 1:7*

And all are justified freely by his grace through the redemption that came by Christ Jesus. — *Romans 3:24*

Therefore, the promise comes by faith, so that it may be by grace and may be guaranteed to all Abraham's offspring — not only to those who are of the law but also to those who have the faith of Abraham. He is the father of us all. — *Romans 4:16*

But the gift is not like the trespass. For if the many died by the trespass of the one man, how much more did God's grace and the gift that came by the grace of the one man, Jesus Christ, overflow to the many! Nor can the gift of God be compared with the result of one man's sin: The judgment followed one sin and brought condemnation, but the gift followed many trespasses and brought justification. For if, by the trespass of the one man, death reigned through that one man, how much more will those who receive God's abundant provision of grace and of the gift of righteousness reign in life through the one man, Jesus Christ! — *Romans 5:15–17*

The law was brought in so that the trespass might increase. But where sin increased, grace increased all the more, so that, just as sin reigned in death, so also grace might reign through righteousness to bring eternal life through Jesus Christ our Lord. — *Romans 5:20–21*

What shall we say, then? Shall we go on sinning so that grace may increase? By no means! We are those who have died to sin; how can we live in it any longer? Or don't you know that all of us who were baptized into Christ Jesus were baptized into his death? — *Romans 6:1–3*

For sin shall no longer be your master, because you are not under the law, but under grace. What then? Shall we sin because we are not under the law but under grace? By no means! — *Romans 6:14–15*

So too, at the present time there is a remnant chosen by grace. And if by grace, then it cannot be based on works; if it were, grace would no longer be grace. — *Romans 11:5–6*

For by the grace given me I say to every one of you: Do not think of yourself more highly than you ought, but rather think of yourself with sober judgment, in accordance with the faith God has distributed to each of you. — *Romans 12:3*

We have different gifts, according to the grace given to each of us. — *Romans 12:6*

The God of peace will soon crush Satan under your feet. The grace of our Lord Jesus be with you. — *Romans 16:20*

I always thank my God for you because of his grace given you in Christ Jesus. — *1 Corinthians 1:4*

By the grace God has given me, I laid a foundation as a wise builder, and someone else is building on it. But each one should build with care. — *1 Corinthians 3:10*

But by the grace of God I am what I am, and his grace to me was not without effect. No, I worked harder than all of them — yet not I, but the grace of God that was with me. — *1 Corinthians 15:10*

Now this is our boast: Our conscience testifies that we have conducted ourselves in the world, and especially in our relations with you, with integrity and godly sincerity. We have done so, relying not on worldly wisdom but on God's grace. — *2 Corinthians 1:12*

All this is for your benefit, so that the grace that is reaching more and more people may cause thanksgiving to overflow to the glory of God.
– 2 Corinthians 4:15

As God's co-workers we urge you not to receive God's grace in vain. — *2 Corinthians 6:1*

But since you excel in everything — in faith, in speech, in knowledge, in complete earnestness and in the love we have kindled in you — see that you also excel in this grace of giving. — *2 Corinthians 8:7*

For you know the grace of our Lord Jesus Christ, that though he was rich, yet for your sake he became poor, so that you through his poverty might become rich. — *2 Corinthians 8:9*

And in their prayers for you their hearts will go out to you, because of the surpassing grace God has given you. — *2 Corinthians 9:14*

But he said to me, "My grace is sufficient for you, for my power is made perfect in weakness." Therefore I will boast all the more gladly about my weaknesses, so that Christ's power may rest on me. — *2 Corinthians 12:9*

I am astonished that you are so quickly deserting the one who called you to live in the grace of Christ and are turning to a different gospel — which is really no gospel at all. Evidently some people are throwing you into confusion and are trying to pervert the gospel of Christ. — *Galatians 1:6–7*

James, Cephas and John, those esteemed as pillars, gave me and Barnabas the right hand of fellowship when they recognized the grace given to me. They agreed that we should go to the Gentiles, and they to the circumcised. — *Galatians 2:9*

I do not set aside the grace of God, for if righteousness could be gained through the law, Christ died for nothing! — *Galatians 2:21*

You who are trying to be justified by the law have been alienated from Christ; you have fallen away from grace. — *Galatians 5:4*

For he chose us in him before the creation of the world to be holy and blameless in his sight. In love he predestined us for adoption to sonship through

Jesus Christ, in accordance with his pleasure and will — to the praise of his glorious grace, which he has freely given us in the One he loves. In him we have redemption through his blood, the forgiveness of sins, in accordance with the riches of God's grace that he lavished on us. — *Ephesians 1:4–8*

But because of his great love for us, God, who is rich in mercy, made us alive with Christ even when we were dead in transgressions — it is by grace you have been saved. And God raised us up with Christ and seated us with him in the heavenly realms in Christ Jesus, in order that in the coming ages he might show the incomparable riches of his grace, expressed in his kindness to us in Christ Jesus. For it is by grace you have been saved, through faith — and this is not from yourselves, it is the gift of God — not by works, so that no one can boast. — *Ephesians 2:4–9*

I became a servant of this gospel by the gift of God's grace given me through the working of his power. Although I am less than the least of all the Lord's people, this grace was given me: to preach to the Gentiles the boundless riches of Christ, and to make plain to everyone the administration of this mystery, which for ages past was kept hidden in God, who created all things. — *Ephesians 3:7–9*

But to each one of us grace has been given as Christ apportioned it. — *Ephesians 4:7*

Grace to all who love our Lord Jesus Christ with an undying love. — *Ephesians 6:24*

It is right for me to feel this way about all of you, since I have you in my heart and, whether I am in chains or defending and confirming the gospel, all of you share in God's grace with me. — *Philippians 1:7*

In the same way, the gospel is bearing fruit and growing throughout the whole world — just as it has been doing among you since the day you heard it and truly understood God's grace. — *Colossians 1:6*

Let your conversation be always full of grace, seasoned with salt, so that you may know how to answer everyone. — *Colossians 4:6*

I, Paul, write this greeting in my own hand. Remember my chains. Grace be with you. — *Colossians 4:18*

We pray this so that the name of our Lord Jesus may be glorified in you, and you in him, according to the grace of our God and the Lord Jesus Christ. — *2 Thessalonians 1:12*

May our Lord Jesus Christ himself and God our Father, who loved us and by his grace gave us eternal encouragement and good hope, encourage your hearts and strengthen you in every good deed and word. — *2 Thessalonians 2:16–17*

The grace of our Lord Jesus Christ be with you all. — *2 Thessalonians 3:18*

The grace of our Lord was poured out on me abundantly, along with the faith and love that are in Christ Jesus. — *1 Timothy 1:14*

To Timothy, my dear son: Grace, mercy and peace from God the Father and Christ Jesus our Lord. *— 2 Timothy 1:2*

He has saved us and called us to a holy life — not because of anything we have done but because of his own purpose and grace. This grace was given us in Christ Jesus before the beginning of time, but it has now been revealed through the appearing of our Savior, Christ Jesus, who has destroyed death and has brought life and immortality to light through the gospel. *— 2 Timothy 1:9–10*

You then, my son, be strong in the grace that is in Christ Jesus. *— 2 Timothy 2:1*

The Lord be with your spirit. Grace be with you all. *— 2 Timothy 4:22*

For the grace of God has appeared that offers salvation to all people. *— Titus 2:11*

But when the kindness and love of God our Savior appeared, he saved us, not because of righteous things we had done, but because of his mercy. He saved us through the washing of rebirth and renewal by the Holy Spirit, whom he poured out on us generously through Jesus Christ our Savior, so that, having been justified by his grace, we might become heirs having the hope of eternal life. *— Titus 3:4–7*

But we do see Jesus, who was made lower than the angels for a little while, now crowned with glory and honor because he suffered death, so that by the grace of God he might taste death for everyone. — *Hebrews 2:9*

Let us then approach God's throne of grace with confidence, so that we may receive mercy and find grace to help us in our time of need. — *Hebrews 4:16*

How much more severely do you think someone deserves to be punished who has trampled the Son of God underfoot, who has treated as an unholy thing the blood of the covenant that sanctified them, and who has insulted the Spirit of grace? — *Hebrews 10:29*

See to it that no one falls short of the grace of God and that no bitter root grows up to cause trouble and defile many. — *Hebrews 12:15*

Do not be carried away by all kinds of strange teachings. It is good for our hearts to be strengthened by grace, not by eating ceremonial foods, which is of no benefit to those who do so. — *Hebrews 13:9*

But he gives us more grace. That is why Scripture says: "God opposes the proud but shows favor to the humble." — *James 4:6*

Concerning this salvation, the prophets, who spoke of the grace that was to come to you, searched intently and with the greatest care, trying to find out the time and circumstances to which the Spirit of Christ in them was pointing when he predicted the sufferings of the Messiah and the glories that would follow. — *1 Peter 1:10–11*

Therefore, with minds that are alert and fully sober, set your hope on the grace to be brought to you when Jesus Christ is revealed at his coming. — *1 Peter 1:13*

Each of you should use whatever gift you have received to serve others, as faithful stewards of God's grace in its various forms. — *1 Peter 4:10*

And the God of all grace, who called you to his eternal glory in Christ, after you have suffered a little while, will himself restore you and make you strong, firm and steadfast. — *1 Peter 5:10*

With the help of Silas, whom I regard as a faithful brother, I have written to you briefly, encouraging you and testifying that this is the true grace of God. Stand fast in it. — *1 Peter 5:12*

Grace and peace be yours in abundance through the knowledge of God and of Jesus our Lord. — *2 Peter 1:2*

But grow in the grace and knowledge of our Lord and Savior Jesus Christ. To him be glory both now and forever! Amen. — *2 Peter 3:18*

NOTES

1. Thomas C. Oden, *The Transforming Power of Grace* (Nashville, TN: Abingdon Press), 33.
2. See Luke 15:11–32.
3. See www.babycenter.com. Data compiled from yearly list of all applications for Social Security numbers in the United States (accessed July 10, 2014).
4. All interviews, unless otherwise noted, were conducted by Lee Strobel and edited for conciseness, clarity, and content.
5. "Luis Palau," available at www.palau.org/about/leadership/luispalau (accessed January 12, 2014).
6. See Proverbs 1:7; 1:32; 10:18; 10:21; 10:23; 12:23; 14:3; 14:8; 14:9; 15:5; 17:21; 23:9; 30:32.
7. "Will You Say Grace?" from sermonindex.net, available at http://www.sermonindex.net/modules/newbb/viewtopic.php?topic_id=44776&forum=35&6 (accessed July 10, 2014). John J. Parsons, "Grace after Meals," Hebrew for Christians, http://www.hebrew4christians.com/Blessings/Daily_Blessings/Food_Blessings/Grace_After_Meals/grace_after_meals.html (accessed September 9, 2014).
8. See Matthew 4:19.
9. Andrew Palau, *The Secret Life of a Fool* (Brentwood, TN: Worthy, 2012), 85-88. For the story of Luis Palau's conversion, see: Luis Palau, *Say Yes!* (Portland, OR: Multnomah, 1991), 31–34.
10. "A thief comes only to steal and to kill and to destroy. I have come so that they may have life and have it in abundance" — Jesus in John 10:10 (HCSB).
11. See Luke 18:18–30.
12. "He who began a good work in you will carry it on to completion until the day of Christ Jesus" (Philippians 1:6).
13. Romans 12:1–2. Steve went on read verse 3: "For by the grace given me I say to every one of you: Do not think of yourself more highly than you ought, but rather think of yourself with sober judgment, in accordance with the faith God has distributed to each of you."
14. See Psalm 103:12; Hebrews 8:12; and 1 John 1:9.
15. See John 8:36.
16. See www.palau.org.

17. Robert D. Putnam and David E. Campbell, *American Grace: How Religion Divides and Unites Us* (New York: Simon & Schuster, Inc.), 10.
18. See John 4:1–26.
19. Luke 5:8: "Simon Peter … fell at Jesus' knees and said, 'Go away from me, Lord; I am a sinful man!'" The use of "Lord" here connotes great respect; in this context, it lacks full confessional force. See translator's note for this verse in *The NET Bible*.
20. See Luke 15:11–24.
21. See Gene Reeves, translator, *The Lotus Sutra: A Contemporary Translation of a Buddhist Classic* (Somerville, MA: Wisdom Publications, 2008), 142–145.
22. See John 1:17.
23. Interview conducted by Jesse Florea at Wind River Ranch in Estes Park, Colorado, originally for publication in *Focus on the Family Clubhouse* magazine. Edited for conciseness, clarity, and content. Used with permission from Focus on the Family.
24. See 2 Corinthians 5:20.
25. See 2 Corinthians 12:8–10.
26. Nic Dunlop, *The Lost Executioner* (New York: Walker Publishing Co., 2006), 189.
27. David Chandler, *Voices from S-21* (Berkeley: University of California Press, 1999), vii.
28. Ibid., 3.
29. Dunlop, *The Lost Executioner*, 19.
30. Ibid., 23.
31. Duch's given name has been variously reported in articles and books. However, Christopher LaPel provided me with a photocopy of Duch's own writing, in which he clearly spells out his name as Kaing Guek Eav.
32. Mary Murphy, "Is There Anything God Can't Forgive?" *Purpose-Driven Magazine* (February 21, 2012).
33. Dunlop, *The Lost Executioner*, 254–262.
34. Ibid., 279, 254.
35. Dunlop describes their meeting with Duch in: Nick Dunlop, *The Lost Executioner*, 267–278. Thayer recounts the experience at http://natethayer.typepad.com.
36. Adrienne S. Gaines, "Notorious Cambodian Killer Seeks Forgiveness," *Charisma* (April 2, 1999).

37. Francois Bizot, "My Savior, Their Killer," *The New York Times* (February 17, 2009).
38. "School Bus Safety Data," from the National Academy of Sciences, U.S. Department of Transportation, and school transportation industry, available at http://www.stnonline.com/resources/10-safety/786-school-bus-safety-data (accessed August 19, 2014).
39. Last name withheld, because at the time of writing Jeremy was still a minor.
40. *The Today Show*, interview with Ann Curry from April 12, 2012.
41. Interview conducted by James Holt, originally for publication in *Focus on the Family Clubhouse* magazine, October 2012. Edited for conciseness, clarity, and content. Used with permission from Focus on the Family.
42. See Matthew 14:25–32.
43. See John 18:10.
44. See John 18:15-27.
45. See Matthew 5:15–16.
46. See Acts 2:41.
47. I recount this story in *God's Outrageous Claims* (Grand Rapids, Michigan: Zondervan, 1997), 248–249.
48. See Luke 23:32–43 for the whole story.
49. John H. Coe is director of the Institute for Spiritual Formation at the Talbot School of Theology. The essentials of the prayer that Kyle took me through, and even some of the wording, were adapted from Coe's various writings. For instance, see: John H. Coe, "Prayer of Recollection in Colossians," www.redeemerlm.org/uploads/1/2/0/7/12077040/prayer_of_recollection.pdf (accessed February 11, 2014) and "Prayer of Recollection," http://wheat-chaff.org/spiritual-development/spiritual-formation/prayer-of-recollection (accessed February 9, 2011).
50. See Romans 10:13–15.
51. Max Lucado, *Grace* (Nashville, TN: Thomas Nelson, 2012), 192, citing Matthew 10:8.

Case for ... Series for Kids from Lee Strobel

Case for a Creator for Kids, Updated and Expanded

Lee Strobel

You meet skeptics every day. They ask questions like:

Are your science teachers wrong?

Did God create the universe?

Is the big bang theory true?

Here's a book written in kid-friendly language that gives you all the answers.

Packed full of well-researched, reliable, and eye-opening investigations of some of the biggest questions, *Case for a Creator for Kids* uses up-to-date scientific research to strengthen your faith in God's creation.

Pick up a copy at your favorite bookstore or online!

Case for ... Series for Kids from Lee Strobel

Case for Faith for Kids, Updated and Expanded

Lee Strobel

You meet skeptics every day. They ask questions like:

Why does God allow bad things to happen?

Can you have doubts and still be a Christian?

Here's a book written in kid-friendly language that gives you all the answers.

Packed full of well-researched, reliable, and eye-opening investigations of some of the biggest questions you have, *Case for Faith for Kids* is a must-read for kids ready to explore and enrich their faith.

Pick up a copy at your favorite bookstore or online!

Case for ... Series for Kids from Lee Strobel

Case for Christ for Kids, Updated and Expanded

Lee Strobel

You meet skeptics every day. They ask questions like:

Was Jesus really born in a stable?

Did his friends tell the truth?

Did he really come back from the dead?

Here's a book written in kid-friendly language that gives you all the answers.

Packed full of well-researched, reliable, and eye-opening investigations of some of the biggest questions you have, *Case for Christ for Kids* brings Christ to life by addressing the existence, miracles, ministry, and resurrection of Jesus of Nazareth.

Pick up a copy at your favorite bookstore or online!

ZONDERkidz™